THE HARVEST

The Bell Witch Series Book 1

Written by Sara Clancy
Edited by Kathryn St. John-Shin

ISBN: 9781072465669
Copyright © 2019 by ScareStreet.com

SCARE STREET

All rights reserved. This book or any portion thereof may not be reproduced or used in any manner whatsoever without written permission from the publisher except for the use of brief quotations in a book review.

This is a work of fiction. Any resemblance to actual persons, living or dead, or actual events is purely coincidental.

Thank You and Bonus Novel!

I'd like to take a moment to thank you for your ongoing support. You make this all possible! To really show you my appreciation for purchasing this book, **I'd love to send you a full-length horror novel in 3 formats (MOBI, EPUB and PDF) absolutely free!**

Download your full-length horror novel, get free short stories, and receive future discounts by visiting www.ScareStreet.com/SaraClancy

See you in the shadows,
Sara Clancy

Chapter 1

The Winthrop Family

Nightshift at the Stonebridge State Hospital for the Criminally Insane always carried an expectant silence. Having done his training at a private mental hospital, Cadwyn had grown used to a constant white noise of rambling whispers, broken sobs, and an endless shuffle of restless bodies. It was different here. After a certain hour, the commotion faded into silence, leaving Cadwyn's footsteps to echo down the seemingly endless hallways. No one was deluded enough to think this calm meant anything good. There was always lingering anticipation. The staff could only wait with bated breath to see what the inmates would present them with next.

Rounding a corner, he braced one shoulder on the heavy iron door and waved lazily at the camera mounted near the ceiling. The deadbolt gave a heavy thunk and the magnetic locks disengaged with a droning buzz.

"You're supposed to check my identification card," Cadwyn reminded the head nurse as he pushed his way into the room.

From the outside, Stonebridge's floorplan seemed pretty straight forward; just a long rectangle of red brick. Inside, however, it was a nightmare. All four floors were divided up by a maze of hallways. Windows were scarce, making it hard for someone to orientate themselves and near impossible to hold onto any sense of time. Mercifully, the unbreakable plastic shielding the rows of fluorescent lights muffled their constant hum. Numerous nurses' stations speckled the building. They, more than anything else, marked the transition from one level of security to the next.

"I know who you are, Cad. And I could see from the numerous cameras that you were all alone," Michelle's voice drifted out from behind the sheet of bulletproof glass. "Of course, I'll make sure to check your credentials before you head into high security."

Cadwyn braced one forearm on the little ledge outside the glass. "Why would I be doing that? I'm on low-risk tonight, remember? First time in months."

A smile slowly stretched Michelle's freckled face. Cadwyn groaned.

"Can't I just have one shift where no one tries to spit on me?"

"Wrong profession, love." Michelle slipped a hand through the small gap in the window and proceeded to wiggle a specimen cup around. "It's time for Peter the Human Eater to have his checkup."

"How many times can one human being have a urinary tract infection?" Cadwyn asked.

"Maybe it's karma," Michelle mused.

"I think the punishment for consuming human flesh would be a bit more than a sore crotch." He snatched the cup away as his friend started to hit him with it. "And why do I have to get the sample?"

"You're on shift."

"So are you. And, according to that wonderfully useful board behind you, there are actually several people here tonight who are assigned to high security."

Michelle shrugged. "None of us are six foot."

"Sayid is."

"He can't do that scary thing you do with your eyes."

Cadwyn chuckled, "What thing?"

"Yeah. Not buying it. Stop looking at me and go intimidate the serial killer into pissing himself, please."

As Cadwyn turned, he noticed an amendment made to the whiteboard. It stopped him in an instant.

"You put Gould back on my rotation?"

Michelle sighed. "Come on, don't make this difficult."

"I told you I wouldn't deal with him."

"Look, I know he rubs you the wrong way. But this place isn't exactly filled with nice people. Besides, you're a nurse. You don't get to pick your patients."

"Michelle, I'm telling you this knowing full well you can have me fired, ruin my reputation, and possibly have my license revoked." He waited for a heartbeat longer than necessary to make sure he had the head nurse's full attention. "If you keep Gould in my rotation, I will kill him."

"Don't even joke like that."

He stared at her until she met his gaze again. "I will do everything in my power to ensure his wound festers. I'll help the infection spread to his bloodstream. I'll watch him die a slow and painful death without ever intervening. Do you understand me?"

At first, Michelle tried to stare him down. She soon gave up. Growling through clenched teeth and snatching a clipboard off its hook with more force than necessary did little to dispel her resentment.

"Fine. I'll take him off. But we never had this conversation. Do you understand *me*?"

"Of course, I do. You're very articulate."

She sneered at him, halfway between amused and enraged, and shoved the clipboard through the narrow gap. A pen followed later for Cadwyn to begin filling it all out. The fact that every pen in the building had to be accounted for at all times really slowed down the paperwork side of things.

She swiped angrily at the board. "Okay, this time you're going to give me a dang answer."

"When have I not?"

"What is it with you and Gould?" she continued, her glare the only sign she had heard his comment. "It's not like he's the worst we've got around here."

Without looking up from his paperwork, Cadwyn replied, "My uncle once told me everyone has pressure points. Some you'll grow out of. Some you'll learn how to deal with. But there will always be something that cuts you right down to your soul."

Michelle scoffed. It was only once Cadwyn looked at her from under his lashes that she shrugged.

"I don't have any."

"My uncle would say you just haven't been tested."

Michelle looked somewhat offended by that but, instead of arguing the point, went back to her whiteboard.

"A wise man knows his weaknesses as well as his strengths," Cadwyn mumbled.

"Oh? Your uncle gave you that pearl of wisdom as well?"

"My grandmother," he answered.

"Right." She rolled her eyes. Scribbling on the whiteboard, she absently asked, "So, your point is that Gould pushes on one of your pressure points?"

Cadwyn cringed. "Cruelty to dogs and pulling teeth."

Michelle's marker left a streak of bright blue across the board as she whirled on him. "Are you kidding me? Teeth? Really? We've got three other patients in this wing alone who did unspeakable things with corpses, and *teeth* is where you draw the line?"

"There's no shame in having pressure points, only in denying them," Cadwyn said under his breath.

She stared at him. "Kimberly fed radioactive material to children."

"Which is horrific and disgusting," he replied. "This isn't a moralistic issue, Michelle. I'm not trying to say my personal pressure points are the epitome of evil. Think of it more like phobias. It's simply something you don't have any control over."

"Teeth?"

"Pulling teeth. Or breaking them. Anything along those lines." He let the conversation drop as his stomach began to churn.

Her frustration was starting to show. Shaking her head, she left her task and returned to the little window that separated them.

"What's any of this got to do with Gould? He's in here because he declared everyone at the IRS to be lizard people and tried to blow up the headquarters."

"Look up what he did to his pet boxer."

"Oh, it was the cruelty to animals button he pushed."

Cadwyn slid the paperwork back to his friend.

"It's cruelty to dogs in particular," he corrected. "And Gould hit both buttons."

Deciding that prolonging the conversation ran the risk of making him physically ill, Cadwyn held up the specimen cup in farewell and stalked down to the next door. With a sweet smile, Michelle refused to open the door until she had personally checked his identification card.

When at last he was through the first door, he quickly ran into the next. Several checkpoints turned the relatively short walk into a string of capsules. Some had a living guard to usher him on his way. At others, he had to flash his credentials to the mounted cameras and wait for someone in a distant room to hit the lock release. Having never worked at the general prison, he sometimes wondered how different their security was. They had hardened criminal psychopaths as well, after all. Although, he supposed the ones who called Stonebridge home were of a different breed.

Two burly guards met him at the last checkpoint. While Cadwyn was slightly taller than both Ted and Steve, each guard easily surpassed him in sheer muscle mass. Ted combined his impressive bulk with a standard issue military hair cut to look more imposing. Steve, on the other hand, achieved the same effect with the array of tattoos that seemingly covered everything but his face. Together, they were an intimidating sight, and that was the whole point.

"A urine sample? Didn't we just do this?" Ted asked, reviewing the notes on the monitor enclosed in the wall.

"It's a follow-up," Cadwyn said.

Steve scratched at the monotone skull tattoo that covered the right side of his neck. "If he throws it at me again, you owe me a beer."

"How is it my fault?" Cadwyn asked, positioning himself between the two men as they started down the long stretch of hallway.

"It ain't. I just want free beer."

"Stay classy," Ted mumbled.

Peter was one of the patients that had to be kept in permanent isolation. Unless absolutely necessary, he wasn't brought out of his cell and no one went in. All the guards hated the few occasions that made it unavoidable. Peter was an opportunistic predator and fond of blitz attacks. It made him unpredictable, volatile, and inclined to keep fighting until he was either sedated or unconscious. The paperwork those encounters created took hours to complete. Everyone hated dealing with Peter.

The final door opened with a loud buzz. Ted pushed the door open. Terrified screams rolled down upon them like a tsunami. Steve pushed Cadwyn behind him before they sprinted forward, silently instructing the nurse on exactly how far away he was allowed to venture. Ted used the radio from his belt to call in the disturbance. A protocol that guaranteed backup would be on the way while also ensuring the wing would go into lockdown. The large slabs of unbreakable glass set in each door allowed Cadwyn to see into each cell as they passed. Some cursed at them. Or spat. A few fed off Peter's panic, using it to fuel their own frenzies. Others hid. A flash of color streaked across his peripheral vision. The passing illusion of a child. A little girl dressed in green. Cadwyn lurched to a stop. *It's too soon.* The thought shattered as Steven bellowed at him. Breaking into a run again, Cadwyn soon caught up, repeating to himself all the while, *it's not midnight. I still have time. I didn't bring her here.*

Peter pressed himself against the door, his voice cracking as he shrieked, his hands smearing blood across everything he touched. The guards increased their speed, effortlessly falling into formation. Ted positioned himself between the door and Cadwyn while Steve moved to the door. Cadwyn was forced to stretch his neck to see over the rounded muscles that lined Ted's shoulders. Peter hadn't left his position but the quickly thickening layer of blood made it harder to see him.

"Back away!" Steve growled, one hand clasping the hilt of his baton. "Back away from the door, now!"

"Let me out!" The words clashed together as Peter repeated them, becoming gibberish and mangling the few others he shoved in at random.

Dread burned behind Cadwyn's ribs. "Did he just say there's a girl in his cell?"

The guards shared a glance before they shifted into breach position. Going in with only two of them wasn't something either wanted to do. But they were quickly passing the point where what they wanted held any weight. Peter was working the whole ward into a frenzy and, judging by the amount of blood painting the door, was in danger of bleeding out. Ted rose up onto his toes, shifting slightly, seeking out a way to see through the few gaps still unstained by crimson. A visible jolt ran through his body. His broad shoulders tensed and, in a flash of movement, he had his baton at the ready and was snarling into his radio.

"Get here, now!"

"ETA in five minutes," came the crackling response.

"Inmate 364 has a civilian in his cell," Ted bellowed over the rising chaos around them. "Repeat. Inmate 364 has a child in his cell!"

"How is that possible?" Steve asked, pushing closer to the glass. The color drained from his face.

"Help me!" Peter's screams broke each time he threw his whole body against the door. "You can't leave me in here with her! Help me!"

The guards ignored the flood of questions that came across the radio to share a shocked glance. At the pause, Peter became more frantic, his actions feeding the confusion. Cadwyn's skin turned to ice when Peter shifted. It was just for a second, but he saw her. A little girl in green.

"Get him out of there," Cadwyn breathed.

The order, while softly spoken, was enough to snap the guards out of their daze. Neither of their extensive training had prepared them for this scenario.

"Let me out! Keep her away from me!"

Cadwyn stepped forward before he could stop himself, his hands balled into fists at his side. Guilt bubbled within his veins. *I didn't pay attention to the time. It's past midnight. I brought her here.* The guards shared a single nod. Steve grabbed the handle, swiped his key card over the sensor, and paused with his hand poised over the keypad.

"Opening in three, two, one."

The door was yanked open with enough force to spray the walls with blood. The sight of the bright red flecks whipped the trapped inmates into a frenzy, spiraling the situation further beyond their captor's control. The noise was deafening. Animalistic screams mingled with demented threats and the constant pounding against the walls. Caught in the middle of it all, Cadwyn was forced to remember just how dangerous the men around him were. He prayed the doors would hold as his muscle memory took over, making him back away, putting the solid wall to his back, and giving the guards room to grapple Peter to the ground.

"You're not listening to me," Peter wailed, thrashing against Ted's hold. "Get me away from her! You can't leave me with her!"

Ted pressed his knee between Peter's shoulder blades, pinning the man to the ground by weight alone.

"Hands above your head, now!" Ted snarled.

Peter's response was to throw his weight to the side, blindly throwing out blood-soaked fists. The noise around them grew impossibly louder.

"Cad!" Steve snapped from where he lay upon Peter's legs, trying to stop the madman from injuring himself. "We've got him! Check on the kid!"

A wall of guards powered down the hallway toward them. *Go now, before they see.* The internal command pushed him into motion. Cadwyn slipped around the three men, careful not to touch the bloody walls as he crossed the threshold. All the while, he prayed to find the child inexplicably inside.

"Cad? What's going on?" Steve asked.

Cadwyn swallowed thickly. "The room's empty."

"What? How? I saw her," Ted demanded in the same instant Steve latched onto one of Peter's arms and pulled it back, stopping only when the joint lingered on the brink of shattering.

"Where did she go?" Steve growled. "What did you do to her?"

The other guards finally joined them, allowing Ted the luxury of turning to catch Cadwyn's eyes.

"She has to be in there. Go and check."

Before Cadwyn could respond, the new arrivals began a chorus of reasons why a child could never get into the cell.

"I know what I saw!" Steve puffed out his barreled chest, challenging anyone to correct him again.

A constant clatter erupted amongst them. The inmates raged, the guards sniped at each other, and all the while, Peter pleaded not to be put back in the cell. 'Not with her.' The repeated demand was the only proof the two guards could point to that they weren't delusional. Until that moment, Cadwyn had held tight to the hope it wasn't *her*. But hearing the fear in the cannibal's voice, seeing the way he had shredded his fingers to the bone in desperation to get away from her; there was only one person he knew who could strike that depth of fear into someone like Peter Wallas.

"What did she look like?" Steve asked Peter, using the response as another shred of proof.

"Dark hair," Peter gasped. "Green dress. Her smile."

The description ended there. Becoming nothing more than broken sobs and endless begging to be taken away.

"That's her," Steve said.

Ted nodded, "That's who I saw."

Cadwyn noticed no one asked him. For the moment, he had been forgotten. It wouldn't last. Soon, they would calm down enough to need someone to tend to Peter's wounds. *Move now*. He had barely taken a single step into the room when he heard it. The arguments drifted away, replaced by the soft, metallic ting of an old music box. The tune was repetitive and simple. A lullaby he knew well. It had taunted his family line for generations. *Find it!* The cell was small and bare. There was nowhere in the blood-stained room for it to hide.

"Cad, get out here. We need you."

He didn't instantly recognize the speaker, but he turned toward the voice. Something solid knocked against his foot. A box about the size of his palm slid over the blood-slicked floor. Constructed from polished wood and glistening metal, it gave the impression of being a solid whole. But, as he watched, the variety of slates squirmed slowly around each other. A steady slide and clack. The timer had already begun its countdown. Cadwyn swooped down and snatched it up, palming it as best he could to keep it out of the guards' sight.

"I need the medic bay." *I can hide the box there.*

Steve and Ted grabbed Peter's arms. Together, they practically dragged him down the hallway, following close behind the lead guards. Two remained, impatient for Cadwyn to move. Before he could leave the room, a disembodied voice drifted to him. An aged whisper. Old and crackling and horrifically recognizable. *Come home, Winthrop. Come home.*

Chapter 2

The Crane Family

Willimina Crane. Reading her own name at the top of the college acceptance letter never got old. Each time brought a new little thrill. Pennsylvania State University wanted her. *Would have been better if it was 'Mina.'* She quickly chastised herself for the thought. What they called her didn't matter. Not until they were putting her name on her diploma, that is. *At least they didn't try and 'correct' it to Wilhelmina,* she thought. *Have to celebrate those small victories, too.*

She bit the insides of her cheeks to keep her growing smile from showing. The paper she held concealed under the table was proof she had achieved the second step of her Life Plan. Not only did she graduate high school with a 4.0 grade point average, but she also got accepted into the best Criminal Justice program in the country.

Then it's on to Harvard Medical School for my doctorate, she recited to herself. Admittedly, things got a little murky from there. She had repeated the question so many times it had almost become a time-killing game. *Practice medicine for a few years first, or head straight to the Federal Bureau of Investigation?* It was so easy to picture both options. Fingers tightening around her acceptance letter, she indulged in a few fantasies. *How long would it take to become a world-renowned surgeon?*

The question hovered in her mind as she glanced around the dining room. Generally, it was a rather large space, with ample room to fit the huge antique dining table her father took an inordinate amount of pride in. Now that almost every blood relative she had was crammed into the room, it suddenly looked rather tiny. The humid air was dense with all the lingering scents of their buffet.

A half dozen bowls still scattered the table top, allowing people to pick at the leftovers. The poker game taking up the far-right end of the table was entering its fourth hour and a *Jenga* tower clattered down to a chorus of cheers. Larger conversations had run their course and those still in the mood to chat were left with a steadily decreasing pool of options. Mina briefly listened in on her sister's argument with one of their cousins. It had been forty minutes and they were still at odds over who would win in a fight between a sasquatch and a leprechaun. She longed to leave the room for at least a little while, get some fresh air, and stretch her legs. *Maybe mom will let me go check on the kids*, she thought, eyeing the door to the living room.

The layout of the house kept the small herd of children in clear view. A cartoon played on the T.V., but no one was left awake to watch it. The few younger teens left to watch over the kids were preoccupied with their phones. Ready to graduate from high school, Mina had finally earned her place at the 'grown-ups' table. She was officially an adult in the eyes of her family and was expected to stay awake with them to see who The Witch selected. *The Witch*. The thought alone made her want to pinch the bridge of her nose. Somewhere along the way, her ancestors had decided the ghost of Katrina Hamilton was stalking them. *A ghost witch*. She mulled the concept over once again. *Yep. Still doesn't make sense.*

Admittedly, the Crane family had experienced some bad luck. Mina couldn't deny that. But a few accidents and a handful of coincidences didn't automatically mean the occult was involved. Mina had tried to prove this point a few times by dissecting the deaths most commonly used by the Crane elders as proof. It hadn't gone over well. No one wanted to be told they had spent their entire lives afraid of strange but completely natural phenomena. That everything they knew to be true was simply a product of mass hysteria and self-fulfilling prophecies.

So here I am, Mina thought as she scanned the room again. A small pang of guilt weaved around her stomach. It seemed ungrateful and even rude not to fall in line. Belief in The Witch was the only thing her family really asked of her after giving so much. *It was just one night of the year, after all. Like waiting up for Santa Claus.* She grimaced.

What kind of jerk makes fun of her loved ones' fear? Even as she reprimanded herself, Mina couldn't shake the thought that it was an accurate comparison. Sooner or later, someone would have to actually intervene to keep the delusion going. Her parents had to put the presents under the tree. And someone would have to make the selection. For the first time, she would actually be in a position to see who's in charge. They might even let her in on the way they helped the situation along. Butterflies flopped around inside her stomach. *That's going to be such an awkward conversation.*

The exaggerated sounds of the cartoon wafted into the dining room, creating a constant backdrop to the low murmur of conversations happening around her. It drew her attention back over to the couch. Last year, she had been one of the teens watching over the little ones. She knew they wouldn't have gone through all of the junk food they had been supplied with. Making a mental note to search through the wreckage on the way back, she resolved to take a trip to the bathroom. Standing as discreetly as she could didn't stop everyone in the room from instantly snapping around to face her. The silence was almost a physical thing.

"Sorry," she mumbled. "I'm just going to duck to the bathroom. I'll be right back."

"Take Jeremiah with you." Her mother's passing command brought life back into the room.

Everyone went back to what they were doing, their chatter sounding louder after the momentary silence. No one was paying enough attention to her to notice the slump of her shoulders.

Seventeen-years-old and I'm still not allowed to walk down a hallway without my older brother's protection, she thought.

Mina carefully kept her mind away from the world of awkwardness that awaited them once they were actually inside the bathroom. There wasn't any point. Privacy didn't exist during The Selection. For the entire twenty-four hours, no Crane by blood was to be out of sight for any reason. It left Mina grateful The Selection happened during the fall. California could be merciful in the summer and Anaheim wasn't too bad. But their air-conditioning had been broken for years, and everyone was always too paranoid to crack open a window on that day of all days. The only thing that could make the stifling heat of the dining room worse would be the collective body odor of her entire extended family.

Mina's hesitation drew her mother's attention.

"It's alright, dear. Jer doesn't mind. Do you sweetie?"

Jeremiah was already by the door, hands shoved into his pockets. "Nah, I wanted to grab my phone charger from my room anyway. We'll get it on the way back."

Whatever protest Mina might have been able to muster died the moment her mother grabbed her forearm and gave it a little squeeze. A fine tremble ran along the podgy digits.

"You'll be okay. Just be quick. Jer will keep you safe."

Mina summoned a small smile. *This is the year,* she told herself as determination rushed through her. The whole night, she had been torn between submitting to the demands of her family and taking another shot at inserting some sanity into the situation. But she knew she couldn't take this much longer. Every year, she helplessly watched her loved ones cower from shadows and legend.

I'm going to finish this tonight. I'm going to make them see the truth.

A voice in the back of her head reminded her facts and figures didn't matter much to those around her. *I'll have to catch them while they're planting the box.*

"Yo, Mina," Jeramiah snapped her from her thoughts. He swung one arm out into the hallway. "Do you have to pee or not?"

"Yes. Thank you for making that public declaration."

"Oh, no." Jeramiah flipped his head back to better show off the roll of his eyes. "Now people know you have normal bodily functions. The horror."

"It's called dignity. I know you're not exactly familiar with the concept."

Instead of a verbal response, he alternated between jabbing his thumbs down the hallway and clapping his hands like trying to coax over a puppy. *Don't swear in front of dad. Don't swear in front of dad.* The mantra helped her to hold her tongue as she crossed the room. Jeremiah had a skill for knowing exactly when she was on the brink and, of course, exploiting it.

"Who's a good girl?" He cooed as she came closer, careful to keep his voice low enough so their parents wouldn't hear. "You're a good girl. Yes, you are."

It was him pinching her cheek that pushed her over the edge.

"Oh, f–" She caught herself just in time to change it to 'forest green.'

In unison, the siblings turned to catch their father's reproachful gaze. The slip wasn't close enough to an actual swear word to bring down his wrath. But the warning was clear.

"So close," Jeremiah taunted in a whisper.

"Would you just go?"

"I'll get you next time."

Concentrating on his display of maniacal laughter left Jeremiah an easy target. One solid shoulder barge knocked him off his feet, leaving him to topple into the wall in a fit of indignation and hissed curse words.

"What was that?" their father snapped.

They fled into the hallway.

"Do you think we'll ever be too old to be treated like children?" she asked.

Jeramiah barked a laugh. "I'll be coasting as soon as I hit twenty. You, however, will always be his sweet little angel."

"That's not fair."

"Sorry. You're the baby. It's the rules."

Mina scrunched up her mouth and busied herself folding her acceptance letter.

"When do you plan on telling them you got in?" Jeremiah asked.

"I've got it perfectly planned out," she said. "I'm going to yell it out of the taxi window on my way to the airport."

"Flawless."

While the hallway wasn't long, it was still enough to turn the noise of the family into a muffled murmur. Jeremiah began to cast quick looks over his shoulder. His smile remained, but the warmth was quickly draining from it.

"Are you okay?" Mina asked.

He nodded rapidly. "Yeah. Of course."

A few more paces and he abruptly paused. "Did you hear that?"

"Hear what?"

"Nothing," he rushed. "It's nothing. Let's just hurry up before mom starts to worry."

She studied him as they passed by the hall closet and reached the bathroom door. "You really believe there's a witch, don't you?"

His casual shrug didn't take the fear from his face. "Don't you?"

"No. Clearly not. Haven't you been listening to me at all?"

"Oh, come on. How many of us have to end up dead before you get with the program?"

"Accidents and coincidences."

"Yeah, well, there's a lot dad hasn't told you," Jeremiah dismissed.

Mina snapped around to look at him. "Like what?"

"Don't worry about it."

"Jer."

He shook his shoulders as if he could dislodge her suspicions. "Don't get all worked up. You're such a red."

Mina found herself trapped somewhere between annoyance and amusement. "Aren't we too old to be using colors as insults?"

"Says the one who threw some shades of green at me earlier."

A part of Mina wanted to bring the conversation back around. To push her brother a little harder and see just how deep his conviction in The Witch really went. But, seeing as how the banter was taking the tension from his shoulders, she just couldn't bring herself to follow the instinct. So instead, she poorly hid the word 'purple' in a forced cough as she led the way into the bathroom.

"Go orange yourself," he grumbled. "And you're just peeing. I'm not hanging around for you to fix up your hair."

"I wasn't going to."

"Oh." He pressed his lips into a tight line. "Right. Okay."

"What?"

"No, no. It looks good." He bared his teeth in a weird fake smile.

If she didn't start ignoring him now, she would have to prepare for a prank war. Something that was never advisable while using the facilities. So she bit back her pride, held her tongue, and set about her business. The downstairs bathroom was the only one used on the night of The Selection. It was far bigger than the upstairs one, thanks to the architect's whim of attaching it to the laundry room, and the extra square footage allowed the process to be a little less awkward than it otherwise would be.

There's no privacy tonight, she told herself. *Or dignity.*

Jeremiah closed the door behind them and rested his forearms on the top of the dryer, playing with his phone as casually as he could. It gave the illusion they couldn't still clearly see each other. Mina chewed on her bottom lip as she tried and failed to answer nature's calling. It was hard to be a Crane with a shy bladder.

"I've officially got a red bar," Jeramiah declared. "My phone is dying while you're doing nothing. You murderer."

"You're not exactly helping."

"Twelve percent!"

"All right, all right. Hey, order me a pizza, yeah? I've been craving some Hawaiian."

The proceeding argument as to whether or not pineapple belongs on pizza created enough of a distraction for her to do what they had come to do. Soon enough, they were back in the hallway.

"So, we agree," Jeremiah declared. "We get the charger and then order two large pepperoni."

"I said Hawaiian."

"Which is obviously insane, so I vetoed it."

Mina's ready reply shattered into a startled squeal. There was barely time to register the cool hand that had latched onto her forearm before it yanked her violently to the side. The folding door of the closet rattled open, revealing the gaping chasm that had replaced the rows of neatly folded sheets. Instinct brought her free hand up to brace herself for impact. But there weren't any shelves remaining to break her fall. The hand didn't release its iron grip until Mina hit the floor. Behind her, the door snapped shut with a sharp clatter. Her heart thrashed within her chest, beating with a sudden ferocity that left her breathless and dizzy.

"Jer?" Mina swallowed thickly to keep her mounting fear from her voice.

In the muted light, she kept a sharp eye on the walls and ceiling, reassuring herself they hadn't moved any closer. *Deep breaths,* she reminded herself. *Walls don't move. It's just in your head.* The doors remained closed, slicing the light into blurred bars.

"Jer, this isn't funny."

"I'm not doing it," Jeremiah replied.

The feeble doors shook as he yanked on the handle.

"Jer!"

"Mom! Dad!"

It wasn't Jeremiah's bellow that caught her off guard. It was the clear, razor-sharp fear that cut through each word. Scrambling up onto her knees, she threw her weight against the door, careful to drive her shoulder into the joints. The thin door shook but refused to budge. *It should open.* Logic and basic physics dictated it should. *Unless something's pushing on the other side.*

"Jeremiah, get off the door!"

"I'm not on it! Dad! Hurry!"

Snapping around, Mina checked the walls once more. *They haven't moved. Walls don't move.* In defiance of her thoughts, the walls shifted. Every time she looked away or blinked, they lurched closer. Afraid to close her eyes, she slammed both hands against the door, and burrowed her fingers into the grooves between the slats in an attempt to pry them open.

"Open the door!"

"Baby?" Her father's voice echoed toward her as if from a distant place. It was soon lost under the chaos of the others crowding outside the door and her own feral screams.

"Open the door! I can't breathe! Open the door!"

Blood rushed through her ears in a deafening roar. The air grew as thick as tar. What little she could choke down coated her throat and clogged her lungs. Her elbows bashed into the walls as she struggled.

They're too close. Too close.

Static devoured her mind. An almost living buzz, like a swarm of insects were scurrying over the paint and plaster. Cold sweat prickled along her spine. Her hands grew slick as she clawed wildly at the door. The sound of breaking wood was lost under the cries of her family. New slivers of light told her she had broken the slats. Fractured edges sliced into her fingertips as further proof. But the door wouldn't open, and the walls now pushed hard against her shoulders.

"Daddy!" she pleaded. "Please, get me out!"

Dust drifted upon the thick, musky air, barely seen within the muted light. Her vision blurred while her aching muscles became as rigid as stone. All the while, shadows shifted across the slats. Someone demanded they knock down the wall. It was almost lost among her own heavy breathing and the dozens of voices assuring her everything would be okay.

She spotted motion in her peripheral vision. Fingers. Needlelike fingers. Slender and covered with skin so thin the veins and tendons threatened to break free. Fear locked Mina's joints, completely immobilizing her as the impossible hands continued to grow.

Striking like a snake, they turned on her, wrapping around Mina and dragging her back. There wasn't anywhere to go. Her spine struck the far wall with enough force to crack the plaster. Dust gushed down like rain, further distorting the light and detailing the motion of invisible creatures. They scurried around her and then over her legs, crawling up the walls and out of sight. Each time Mina tried to focus on them, to determine their shape and size, the creatures would shake off the dust and completely disappear from sight.

It happened so gradually Mina didn't notice it at first. All the noise from outside the closet drifted away into a series of whispers and sighs. It made the sharp, metallic ping all the louder. The odd notes came without warning, making her jump and push harder back against the wall. It was impossible to move since the sides of the closest were now as narrow as a coffin. Separate notes sped up and joined, becoming a tune. The song of a music box. It drifted to her from the darkness as the ceiling loomed ever closer. The familiar lullaby coursed through her veins like ice water.

Hot, rancid breath gushed over her shoulder. "Come home, Crane. Come home."

Mina screamed. The door burst open, flooding the linen closest with fresh air and light. Thrashing, sobbing, and gulping for air, Mina realized she wasn't stuck in a makeshift casket. Instead, she had somehow crammed herself under the lowest shelf of the closet, wedging her body between the wall and a storage box.

"It's okay, baby," her father said as he grabbed her kicking legs and dragged her out. "Just breathe. You're out now. I have you. Just breathe."

Braced against her father's chest, the rest of her family came in all at once for a singularly crushing hug.

"I'm so sorry, Mina," Jeremiah sobbed. "I didn't see it coming. I'm sorry."

Mina was vaguely aware of her mother snarling, "I told you to watch her."

Her focus was on the music box. She had no memory of picking up the cube that she now clutched in her right hand. But it was there. Solid and real and still playing the lullaby.

"No," her mother whispered.

Jeremiah latched onto her wrist like she was going to be dragged away again at any moment.

"We'll take care of it," her father assured her. "Don't worry. I'll take care of everything."

Chapter 3

The Bell Family

Basheba tore off a chunk of her hamburger meat and tossed it across the car. Buck went for it instantly. The Rottweiler only had to bounce slightly in the front passenger seat to snatch the morsel out of the air. Still, it was enough to spray the interior with his slobber.

Basheba quickly twisted to protect her food. "Really, Buck?"

The words came out as a mixture of a whine and a laugh, which would have only confused the dog if hadn't been so fixated on chomping down his mouthful.

"I know you know how to swallow," she grumbled.

Too lazy to properly clean up the mess right then, she leaned back in her seat and flopped her foot about. She had learned during the past year that thick hiking socks were pretty effective at mopping long trails of drool off of dashboard vinyl. Once done, she left them up on the dash, positioning them over a heater vent. This was one of the benefits of being four-foot-eight. Cramped spaces didn't really make it difficult for her to get comfortable. Licking his chops, Buck shuffled closer until his massive head rested upon her thigh. It was hard for Basheba to be appropriately annoyed at the drool dampening her thermal leggings when he gazed up at her with his big brown eyes.

"You've had your dinner," Basheba dismissed.

It didn't dislodge her dog's head from her lap, but she did at least get to take another bite in peace. Savoring the taste, she relaxed a little more in her seat, eyeing the car's neon clock. *Almost midnight.* It was hard to believe an entire year had passed since she had last been in

Nashville. The area was pretty enough, especially when ravaged by the coming fall. Some trees stood like bare skeletons, their gnarled, twisted branches clutching at the chilled night air. Those that still had their leaves had shed their summer shades for the blazing colors of fall.

While it was bitterly cold, there was still no promise of coming snow. She cocked her head to the side to better study the sky. If they had any luck, the whole week would pass without so much as a flurry. The passing thought made her snort. *Whoever goes in will have a lot more to worry about than the weather.* A chill worked its way down her spine. She nudged the heater higher with her toe. The bounce of her thigh made Buck grumble with annoyance, and she rubbed him with her knuckles as penance.

Generally, she loved winter. Even sleeping in her car hadn't diminished that. All she needed was a good sleeping bag and Buck's body heat. It was just this one week that made her detest the cold—the 23rd to the 30th of October. She resolved to grab another sweater the moment she finished her meal. Stuffing an intact onion ring into her mouth, Basheba looked out over the parking lot.

It was a stroke of luck that her favorite burger joint also happened to be open all night. This way, not only could she get a decent bite to eat at midnight, but she could camp out for the night with little chance of being asked to move along. She rechecked the clock. *Not much longer now.* Soon, Katrina would make her selection. Either Basheba would crawl into the back seat and get some sleep, or she'd begin the forty-minute drive north. Back to Black River. To the place where it all started.

Anticipation prickled her skin like a thousand needles. She began to mindlessly eat, shoving the onions rings into her mouth faster than she could chew, her eyes constantly searching the horizon. Tonight, the environment was everything. She needed to make sure her setting was at least somewhat under her control. Somewhere familiar but not isolated. Populated and busy. Somewhere well-lit with little to obstruct her vision or escape.

She had carefully chosen the parking lot of the diner. Towering floodlights filled the nearly barren space, allowing her to watch the steady stream of people come and go. A mixture of stressed college students and people coming off late-night shifts. The bars were far enough away she wouldn't have to worry about any drunk idiots trying to get into her car. And, if things went bad, the open space would allow her to run for quite a distance before traffic became an issue. The car's windows were up, the doors locked, everything safely stowed away. Scratching Buck behind his ears, Basheba decided she was as prepared as she could hope to be.

Unable to resist the dog's pleading eyes, she gave him the last bit of her hamburger, keeping the onion rings for herself. Alternating between devouring her deep-fried treats and slurping down her soft drink, she continued to scan the area. The night pressed in on the edges of the lights, still and dark as coal. It made it impossible to miss the first light flicking off. The spotlight was situated on the far side of the carpark. Without it, the night rushed a few feet closer to her. It was barely anything, but her heart froze.

Buck's ears flattened as he sat up. His nose twitched and his eyes locked on the distant patch of shadows. They both watched as another light died with a low, electric hiss. The scent of ozone stained the air. Shadows rose up like a surging tide, silent as a serpent. It wrapped around the next light in the row and, with a heavy thud, it died, too.

Darkness rushed forward to claim new territory. It was so dense and complete that it looked as if someone had simply cut chunks of the world out of existence. Basheba watched. Waited. The few remaining floodlights kept her little car nestled within a warm orange glow. The neon sign of the burger joint buzzed like a swarm of bees. People continued to come and go, none of them paying the slightest attention to the abyss that existed about a yard from their feet. Glancing away was her mistake.

The darkness crashed forward, consuming everything in its path, coming to an abrupt stop about a foot from the front of her car. Buck stiffened, shoulders hunching and a low growl rumbling within his broad chest.

"Steady," she whispered to him.

Obediently, he stopped squirming, although his growl remained constant, filling the empty air. Basheba craned her neck to see a little more. Everything was still. The shadows hung before her with razor-sharp precision. She squinted but couldn't find a single shape in its obsidian depths. Carefully, she reached down and turned the high beams on with her oil-slicked fingers.

The darkness peeled back, not fleeing from the headlights in long tunnels. More like a retreating tide, washing back until it revealed a child. Possibly no older than seven, the little girl stood with her hands loosely clasped in front of her, her shoulders down and relaxed, her feet together to give the overall appearance of delicate innocence. The hemline of her floral dress tapped her knees as it drifted in the evening wind. It was the crude mask covering her head that made Basheba cringe.

The dented, peeled dome was forged into a mangled jack-o'-lantern. A deformed smile separated the head. Gaping holes served as eyes. The mask hid all of the girl's features and left Basheba stunned. Buck's throaty growl served as her only anchor to reality. Sinking her fingers into his fur kept her from spiraling down into the throes of panic. It wasn't children in and of themselves that summoned an almost primal fear within her. But when paired with decrepit, old costumes, especially the ones that kept her from seeing their faces, she couldn't control her instinctual reaction. What terrified her the most, however, was there was only one person left in her life who knew of her rather unique phobia.

"Hello, Katrina," Basheba whispered, trying to keep her voice somewhat strong, defiant.

Buck erupted into a series of barks, the sudden noise snapping any bravado she had managed to summon. She jumped. Her startled scream transformed into a gasp as her icy beverage drenched her lap.

The sensation stole her attention for only a split second, barely a flick of her gaze. But when she looked back, the child was gone.

Buck's growl was the only thing to break the silence. Gone were the other people, the cars, the general murmur of life that clustered around the all-night diner. The night had closed in while she had been distracted by the single child. It now pressed in around her on all sides, leaving barely an inch of visibility. Buck lunged up, awkwardly shifting his weight around the passenger seat, his nose twitching wildly as he thrashed about. His attention was drawn to each window in turn.

Long strings of saliva dripped from his jaws as his lips curled back from his fangs. His growls turned into savage barks. Leaping and lurching, he twisted around to try and see each window. Basheba turned with him. Despite her dog's frenzied outburst, it was still possible to hear the sounds drifting in through the locked car doors. Children's laughter came from the darkness. Pattering footsteps circled her like a shark within the murky abyss of the ocean depths. There was no longer just one, but dozens. Each running wild, making it impossible to track any of them by sound. They came with the fluttering snap of streamers.

The first strike against the window caught her off guard. A startled yelp escaped both her and Buck. Both of them whipped around to stare at the rear door but, in seconds, it was as if the skies had opened. The unseen specters burst free of the shadows to strike the car before disappearing once more.

Childish giggles rose louder than Buck's threatening snarls. Each child's head was covered with stacks that could barely be called masks, fitted with molded noses and grotesque frozen smiles. The patches, pale of color, streaked across her vision, followed by long trails of serpentine streamers.

Laughter rang in her ears as footsteps raced across the roof of her car. The vehicle trembled under the force, causing the suspension to squeal. She shrank back against her door, balling herself up tight, avoiding Buck's now aimless attacks. A hand came down against the glass just beside her head. Basheba spun around, her heartbeat choking her as she found a handprint of condensation marring the glass. A new wave of horror pushed everything else into the back of her awareness. Breathing hard, she reached out. Her trembling fingertip smeared the child's handprint. *It's on the inside.*

"Come home, Bell."

Basheba threw herself back from the small voice. Wedged against the steering wheel, the loud bellow of the car's horn broke the night. It covered the sound of the attack but did nothing to diminish the voice of the pumpkin-headed girl. She sat in the back seat, a small living cube of wood and metal set upon her lap, clasped between tiny hands.

"Come home."

The girl stretched out her hand, the box resting upon her fingers in offering. It wasn't possible for Basheba to reach it without moving from her seat upon the horn. Still, when she lifted her hand, the box appeared against her palm. Light burned her eyes. She flinched, and it was all gone. The night had returned to what it had been before, filled with people and cars and life as it had always been. All that remained was the box.

It was just large enough that she had to stretch her fingers to keep it in her palm, and it was cold to the touch. The polished sides were an intricate pattern of glistening metal. As if awakening to her touch, the pieces began to move, sliding and clicking into new positions. Basheba's eyelids fluttered closed as a slow melody filled the air, simple and repetitive, like a child's lullaby. Buck nuzzled his wet nose against her, whimpering with concern. The touch startled her. Suddenly the horn was blaring painfully in her ears. She shifted back into the driver's seat, one hand clutching the box while she rubbed at Buck's neck. He nuzzled into the touch, inching closer until his thick head was pressed against her neck.

"It's okay. We're okay," she whispered.

He didn't believe her. *Smart boy.* Feeling the eyes upon her, Basheba finally managed to take action. She secured the box carefully in the glove box, put on her seatbelt, and peeled the car out onto the main street. Buck kept his head rested upon her forearm as she took the exit to Black River. It was time to go home.

Chapter 4

The Sewall Family

"Ozzie?"

Osgood Davis glanced up from his phone as his mother opened his bedroom door, and froze, trying to look as innocent as humanly possible. It was hard to make the aesthetic look convincing after having been caught in clear defiance of her order to go to sleep. She arched an eyebrow and crossed her arms over her chest, her Manolo Blahnik pumps clicking loudly against the marble hallway floor. It was a clipped sound that had always preceded a grounding. He had always suspected that's why his mother insisted on wearing them in the house. It was all an intimidation technique.

"You were supposed to go to sleep an hour ago."

"I had homework," he declared.

The well-used excuse was his only shot, since his education was the one thing she would put above everything else. He could come down with the black plague and she would still be quizzing him on the periodic table.

"Can't let that fancy private school go to waste," he pressed with a smile.

Her eyes narrowed. "Osgood Davis, don't think for a second you're too old for me to tan your hide."

He blinked at her. It was always a little strange hearing Texas slang with a Korean accent.

"I swear, ma. I was turning in right now."

The tapping continued as she narrowed her eyes. "You better. Or

I'm taking away that phone."

"Got it."

"And your Porsche."

"What?" Ozzie snapped, springing up to give her an appropriately horrified look. "A bit much, don't ya think?"

She scowled. "Ya? Am I raising a yokel?"

"You," he corrected swiftly, barely squeezing the word in before she continued.

"I've never felt comfortable with you having that thing. It's too much power for someone just learning."

"Everyone else has got one, Ma."

"I'd rather you practice on the Mercedes," she dismissed. Releasing a long sigh, she smiled at him, seemingly forgetting all annoyance. "You haven't heard the scratching tonight, have you?"

The question instantly shifted the mood in the room. What had started as an annoyance had become something to keep him up at night. About a week ago, he had first heard the scratching, gnawing sound on the walls of the pool house. He hadn't thought much of it. Dallas, like any major city, wasn't really known for its abundance of nature. So it was pretty common for whatever wildlife around to make their way onto the Davis property, filling up the lakes and running about the spacious lawns. He hadn't thought much of it. That was until he had heard it against the living room wall, then just outside his window on the third floor. Then inside the walls.

They had hired three different pest control companies. None of them had found anything, and the sound had grown worse. Long scrapes that trailed from one side of the room to the other, that crossed above his head while he was trying to sleep.

It probably wouldn't have bothered him half as much if it wasn't for his parents' reactions. Cue a lot of whispering, skulking about, and heated shouting matches with an old family friend, Percival Sewall. That alone was strange; everyone loved Percival.

Ozzie shook his head, dread becoming thick in the pit of his stomach as he watched his mother sigh with relief.

"Good. That's good."

"What am I missing?"

His mother straightened and forced a smile. "Nothing, baba. Nothing but a good night's sleep."

"Do you think that sounds convincing?"

She jabbed one manicured finger in the general direction of his pillow. "Sleep. Now. Or no Porsche."

Ozzie dramatically leaped for the sheets. While the antics managed to coax a laugh out of her, she still didn't give him enough time to get comfortable before turning off the overhead light, leaving him to do the rest of his squirming by the glow emitting from the hallway.

"So you're aware, I will be randomly checking on you later. If I find you awake again, you will feel my wrath."

"Yes, Mom."

With a last parting smile, she closed the door. Ozzie waited until the sound of her heels had completely faded before getting up. The whole trip to the door left him feeling like an idiot. It didn't stop him, though. He cracked the door open, almost sagging with relief as a sliver of light broke into his room, turning the darkness into muted shades of gray. Just barely enough for him to make out the outline of the objects filling his room. It eased the knot in his stomach but didn't take it away completely.

He padded across the carpet, set his iPhone to charge, and got back into bed. After a few moments of staring at the bar of light, he eventually closed his eyes. Just as he drifted toward sleep, he heard it; the scratching of nails against wood. It trailed along the wall, never crossing close enough to the window for him to catch sight of what was making the sound. His heart stammered when the direction shifted. No longer outside. The long, slow scrape came from within the wall by his head.

Ozzie's fingers twisted up the sheets as he listened to it coming closer. Inch by inch. Stopping only when the thin layer of plaster and paint separated them. Then silence. Staring at the ceiling, he held his breath, straining to hear it again. When it came, it was far louder than before. No longer the chipping of wood but the tearing of fabric. It came from the underside of his pillow.

A scream ripped from his throat as he leaped from the bed. He sprinted across the room, snapping on the light in under a second. Panting hard, he stared at his bed, waiting for something to crawl its way out of the mattress.

"Master Osgood?" Maxwell, the family butler asked from somewhere down the hallway.

Ozzie couldn't find his voice to respond. The sound replayed in his mind as he struggled to find some other explanation. But there wasn't one. He knew what he had heard.

Maxwell called for him again from just outside his door. Ozzie huffed a breath and wondered just how much he'd cop from his friends if they ever heard about this. *Almost sixteen and still afraid of the dark.*

"I'm alright, Max. I didn't mean to worry you," Ozzie said, mindlessly swinging one side of the double doors open. "Can you get me some honey tea? I can't sleep."

Leaning back into the hallway, he sought to catch his butler's eyes. Ozzie's stomach plummeted. A few feet still separated him from Maxwell. Each pore of the middle-aged man's body stood out as a pitch-black dot. Every lumbered motion the man took made them split open. Tiny spiders scrambled out of his skin. Millions in number. Birthing only for a new egg to ooze into the vacated pore.

"Master." Maxwell rasped the words around the long, thin arachnid legs that flicked and squirmed past his lips.

The hatchlings flooded across the floor, the walls. They clung to the ceiling and consumed every trace of light as they scurried toward him. Ozzie screamed. The sound barely reached his ears as he turned and sprinted down the hallway. The cool marble floor bit at his feet as he ran. He barreled down the wide, twisting staircase, not daring to touch the railing as the spiders kept pace beside him.

"Mom! Dad!" The words left him breathless.

Missing a step sent him tumbling. The sharp edges of the stairs smacked against him as he rolled, hit the wall, and dropped the last of the distance to the foyer. Panic alone got him back up. Presented with the sprawling estate around him, he didn't know which way to go. Two wings, three levels, and endless corridors. The wrong choice could leave him separated from his parents by a living wall of arachnids.

"Mom! Dad! Help!"

"Master Osgood," Maxwell rattled behind him.

Tiny spiders scrambled over Ozzie's feet. All thought was severed. He sprinted for the door, driven by the single desire to flee, to get away from the monster constantly birthing the eight-legged monstrosities. He flung the front door open and instantly smacked into an immovable wall. Arms locked around him. The confinement sent Ozzie into a wild panic. He thrashed and screamed and struck the wall but couldn't move it.

"You made your point!" Percival yelled.

The sharp roar rumbled from the wall against Ozzie. Shock left him breathless as he snapped his head up. *What is he doing here?* Ozzie pushed the thought aside. It didn't matter why the old family friend was there. It only mattered that he *was*. That Ozzie wasn't alone with Maxwell anymore.

Percival didn't look at him. The balding man's gaze was locked on the staircase, dark eyes burning with hatred as well as fear. Ozzie struggled to get free as the clicking of spider legs echoed in his ears.

"You made your point, Katrina! He'll be there! Leave him alone," Percival continued

The clicking came to a sudden halt, replaced by the soft ping of a music box. Trembling, Ozzie chanced a glance over his shoulder. Maxwell and the swarm that had crawled from his skin were gone, replaced by a small girl who stood halfway up the staircase. She smiled down at them, cradling a cube of wood and metal between her tiny hands. Ozzie was vaguely aware of his parents coming into the room. Their gasps of shock. Their mad dash to get to him. But the little girl held his attention.

"Come home, Sewall." She disappeared but her voice still hovered within the cavernous room. "Come home."

Ozzie couldn't place the exact moment when it happened, but he found himself clutching the box, feeling it twitch as the melody continued to play.

Numb with shock, dizzy from his fading adrenaline rush, he could only think to mumble, "But I'm not a Sewall."

Chapter 5

Ozzie had no idea why his mother had insisted on making him tea. The only way the beverage was going to calm him down was if he used it for a makeshift lobotomy. Still, she insisted. So he sat in awkward silence with Percival as his father got him an ice pack for his head. It hadn't even occurred to him he was injured until his dad had started fussing.

"Ethan," Ozzie's mother said as she placed a mug before his father. She handed the second to Percival.

"Thanks, Ha-Yun," he smiled weakly.

She pursed her lips into a tight smile before going to collect her own mug.

Ethan placed a hand on his son's shoulder, drawing his attention, "Do you need anything for the pain?"

"I'm fine, Pa. Really. It's just..." He shivered and tightened his grip on the mug until his fingers ached. "The spiders. You know? Did you see the spiders?"

"Yeah, I did." Ethan's sharp cheekbones pushed uncomfortably against the top of Ozzie's head as he pulled him into a one-armed hug. "They're gone, son. I promise, they're gone."

Ozzie leaned into the embrace before the thought hit him. "Maxwell! Did anyone check on him?"

"He's okay," Ha-Yun assured, reaching out to squeeze his hand. "He was a bit confused why I had woken him up, but other than that, he's perfectly fine."

Ozzie nodded absently, barely aware of the motion. "Good. That's good."

It seemed as soon as one fear was eased, another question forced itself to the forefront of his mind. He lifted his eyes to meet Percival's dark gaze.

"That thing... Why does it think I'm a Sewall? Was it coming after you? I don't really see how it could confuse us."

He didn't need to do anything to draw attention to the obvious differences between them, but Ozzie still flopped a hand around for good measure. Aside from the apparent age difference and Ozzie's evident Korean heritage, Ozzie's jaw was square but soft, and his eyes carried the same dark shade as his thick black hair. Percival, on the other hand, was a bald, blue-eyed white man, with a short, graying beard and disproportionally dark eyebrows.

"Well, maybe we have similar eyebrows," Ozzie noted.

Percival wiped a hand over his face, but it didn't stop his chuckling.

"Don't get me wrong," Ozzie continued. "You're cute for an old guy. If I look like that at your age, I wouldn't be mad."

"Hahaha! Thanks for that," Percival's said, his voice gruff but soft at the same time.

It was the seriousness in his eyes that made Ozzie blurt out. "I'm not a Sewall."

"Actually," Ha-Yun began before sharply clearing her throat.

Her gaze darted between the two men surrounding Ozzie. Ethan repeated his wife's throat-clearing maneuver, took a deep breath, and turned to Ozzie.

"I'm a Davis," Ozzie insisted. "Osgood Davis."

"You are," Ethan said. Reluctantly, he added, "But not biologically."

Ozzie stared wide-eyed at his father before whipping around to face his mother. "You cheated on dad?"

"I would never!" Ha-Yun snapped.

"They had stopped dating before we got together," Ethan insisted.

"How did she end up with his baby then?"

"Ozzie," Percival soothed. "It's true I was with your mother. It was a summer romance, and I loved her. I still do. But we weren't *in* love."

"So you were happy with her hooking up with your best friend?" Ozzie shrieked.

"I'm the one who set them up," Percival chuckled. "Look at them. They're a perfect match."

"And we always told you that ours was a whirlwind marriage," Ethan continued.

"Did you know you weren't my father?"

"I am your father," Ethan said sharply. "Percival is your godfather."

"Did you decide that, or did you know?"

Ethan looked to Ha-Yun.

"We knew there was a possibility," she said carefully, looking at each man in turn as she continued. "And, after we all sat down and discussed it, we decided we didn't need to know."

"I protested that point."

"Percival..."

"Not because I didn't think you two would be the best parents for him. Hell, I'd be a horrible father. This is the exact reason why I wanted to do the paternity test."

"And it's the exact reason we didn't," Ha-Yun snapped before she caught herself. Deflating with a sigh, she rested her elbows on the table and rested her face in her hands.

"I thought you were insane," she admitted.

"In her defense, we both did," Ethan said. A small smile tipped one corner of his mouth.

Percival shook his head but couldn't keep himself from laughing. "Yeah. I must have sounded nuts. If I was a petty man, I'd be pointing out how right I was."

Unable to decide what to process first, Ozzie settled for shrieking, "What is going on?!"

Percival put a hand up to quiet the other two and took the lead.

"You're going to have to bear with me here. This is information we tell Sewall children from birth. The only other time I had to tell the whole story to someone outside of the family, it obviously didn't go all that well. So, just listen to the whole tale first, okay?"

Ozzie reluctantly nodded, suddenly very grateful to have the mug. It gave him something to latch onto.

"In the early 1800s..."

"1800s? You're starting in the 1800s? How about you just explain what happened eighteen minutes ago?"

"What did I just say about interrupting?" Percival deadpanned, his dark eyebrows lowering over narrowing eyes.

"Sorry."

Hunching his shoulders, Ozzie bit hard on the inside of his lip and struggled to keep his silence.

"We're starting in 1812 in the small Tennessee town of Black River because that's when the Bell family first ran into Katrina Hamilton." Percival's eyes scanned the room as he almost whispered the name, as if he thought the muttering would conjure the girl. "It all started as a property dispute." He huffed a bitter laugh at that. "Katrina sold the Bells some barren land. They made it work. She declared they had swindled her and demanded they give her a percentage of their profits. Understandably, no one took her seriously. They probably would have if they had known she was a witch."

"A witch?" Ozzie blurted out.

"Did that look like a normal occurrence to you?" Percival challenged.

"Yeah, but, come on. Witches? It's just a religion or something, right?"

"Don't mix up witch with wiccan, kiddo. We're not talking about healing herbs or benevolent spirits. What we're dealing with is dark and satanic." He paused to take a sobering breath before continuing. "Katrina proceeded to torment the Bell family for two years. She tried everything she could to ruin them. Socially, financially, spiritually. Anything she could do to them, she did. For two years, she raged a war against them. If it wasn't for the aid of the Winthrop family, the Bells would have been destroyed."

"Okay," Ozzie prompted when Percival fell silent.

"In 1817, two young girls were helping with the fall harvest. Basheba Bell and Caroline Winthrop. Hearing a baby's cry, they looked up to see a cloaked figure taking the Bell infant into the woods. They gave chase, raising the alarm for the field hands to follow. The slaves testified they had the girls and the strange figure in sight until they passed the first line of trees. Then, they all just disappeared. Vanished."

Percival took a drink before continuing.

"Two days later, the girls returned. They accused Katrina Hamilton of witchcraft, and declared she had been stealing children from the town and sacrificing them to the devil in the forest. Now, this was two hundred years after Salem, give or take. Folks liked to think they were too smart to believe in witches anymore. And no one wanted the reputation of being the hick town that hanged a poor woman because of suspicion and hysteria. It was a hard sell. And if it had just been the Bell child, no one would have convicted her. It was the Winthrop girl."

He chuckled.

"That eight-year-old had steel in her blood. Many histories believe that it was her testimony that convinced the judge, appropriately enough named Justice Crane, of Katrina's guilt. She was hanged."

"Hanged?" Ozzie cut in despite his best efforts not to interrupt again. "I thought witches were burned at the stake."

Percival shook him off while simultaneously taking a sip of his tea. "No, we're in America, not Europe."

Ozzie blinked at him.

"They were burned in Europe. There were laws against it in America. Witches were hanged."

"But, the Salem Witch Trials. They burned two hundred people," he insisted.

"No, they didn't," Percival said. "Who the hell taught you history? Two hundred were *accused*. A few died in prison and one man was crushed to death during interrogation, but only nineteen were actually executed. And all of them were hung."

"Oh."

"The burnings happened in Europe. That was a whole different nightmare and, while Katrina was born in Germany, has nothing to do with what I'm telling you. So please, just shut up for five minutes."

Ozzie clamped a hand over his mouth to better illustrate his continued efforts.

"As I was saying, Katrina was hanged. That's when things got worse. It started as scratches."

He managed to keep from blurting anything out by shooting quick glances to his parents. They both avoided his gaze, guilt evident on their faces. *Percival told them it would happen.* The realization came with no trace of resentment. He had heard it, seen it right before his eyes. The box was sitting at the center of the kitchen counter to prove it. And yet, he was still having a hard time believing any of it. Ozzie couldn't imagine what it would have all sounded like for his parents. Just an old friend, an urban legend, and a request to jump on board with the insanity.

Percival continued. "It started on the outside of the farmhouse and, at first, they were convinced it was some kind of animal. Their slaves became concerned it was one of the strange creatures they had reported seeing in the surrounding woods. Then the sound moved inside. I've been told you've experienced something similar."

"Is that why you're here tonight?" Ozzie asked.

"I always keep an eye on you around this time of year. I know that sounds a little on the 'stalker' side of things, but let me finish and I'm sure you'll understand."

Percival took a deep breath and downed half of his quickly cooling tea before he continued.

"You've witnessed it doesn't take long for these kinds of things to escalate. For the Bells, it was moving objects, spontaneous fires, physical attacks, disembodied voices. And it wasn't just them who witnessed it. When word got out, people came from miles around in hopes of seeing proof of a ghost. Like they were some kind of sideshow attraction, like it was entertainment to see a terrified child being thrown across a room. And yes, incidents like that were common and well documented."

Seeing his friend struggling to contain his growing anger, Ethan cut in, "And they believed it was this Katrina Hamilton?"

The question jarred Percival out of his thoughts. "She admitted it. You have to understand the voice they heard wasn't just some distant, unintelligible whisper. It was clear. She held conversations with different visitors. By all accounts, she was also well versed in profanity, which she hurled at the Bells for hours on end. In time, Katrina's influence spread. She was still fixated on the Bell family, but the Winthrops, as well as the Cranes, started to report encounters. The torment continued for four years. Then, in the winter of 1821, she was strong enough to kill."

Ha-Yun lurched off of her stool and headed to the fridge. "I need a drink."

"I don't get one?" Ozzie asked as he watched her pour a generous amount of red wine into three glasses.

"You're fifteen."

"So I'm old enough to get haunted but not old enough to drink?" Ozzie ran a hand through his thick black hair, steadying himself to ask, "I still don't understand why she hates the Sewalls. Or the box." While the cube had mercifully stopped playing its lullaby, there was still life in it. The walls squirmed. Tiny irregular shapes slithered around each other before falling into a new position with a soft click. "Full disclosure; that box creeps me out."

"That's probably because there's a demon inside," Percival said before finishing half of his wine in one large gulp.

"What?" Ozzie shrieked.

Percival held up one finger as he finished off the glass and handed it back to Ha-Yun, who dutifully refilled it.

"Before we get into that... don't worry, we're close... I'll explain how we got dragged into it. Our ancestor, Abraham Sewall, was an old college friend of Justice Crane. Apparently, they were roommates or some such thing. He had just arrived in Black River to help make some sense out of the situation when Griogair Bell was murdered. Katrina probably should have done her research before playing her hand. Abraham had a lot of resources at his disposal. Enough to help the Bells, Winthrops, and Cranes all escape Black River, and Katrina's influence. For the most part, at least. She still got her revenge, still gets to play her games."

Twisting the stem of the wine glass between the fingers of his right hand, Percival reached out to tap one finger against the top of the box.

"We call it the Harvest. It's happened every year on this day since 1821. Katrina will select one member from each of the four families and present them with a demon box. See the way it moves? It's counting down. If nothing's done, it will open seven days exactly from when she handed it to you."

"And unleash a demon?" Ozzie said. "An actual, real demon?"

He nodded. "You'll see it around soon enough. While it's contained, it can't directly cause you any physical harm. But it will mess with your head; show you things, make you hear things that aren't there. Trick you into hurting yourself. Anything it can think of to try and stop you from finding the key and relocking the box."

"Relocking? I can keep it trapped in there?"

"That's the game, Ozzie. If you win, Katrina takes the box back, and you're left with the fallout."

"If I lose?" Ozzie asked.

"You die. Horribly."

Both of his parents crowded closer to him, eyeing the box with horror.

"It's okay," his mother soothed. "We'll help you. We'll find the key."

"We'll be with you every step of the way," his father promised.

"You can't," Percival said, nursing his second round of red wine.

Ha-Yun narrowed her eyes, her painted lips pulling back into a snarl, "I'm not just going to watch my son being tortured and do nothing."

"You don't get to watch, either. Only the selected four can go into the forest during the Harvest."

"What kind of rule is that?" she snapped.

A bone-deep weariness filled Percival's eyes as he replied. "One we didn't pick. Katrina's game. Katrina's rules."

"Well, we won't play by her rules," Ha-Yun said.

"Gee, never thought of that in the almost two-hundred years we've been forced to do this." Rage began to seep into his voice as he tightened his grip on his glass. "Despite what you might think, we do love our family members. None of us want this. We don't offer up our children, our parents, our siblings as sacrifices. We've fought back in every way you could possibly think of. And we've always failed."

"So you do nothing?"

"We teach them!" It was the first time Ozzie had ever heard the placid Percival shout in anger, and it made him jump. "We let them know this is coming and prepare them as best we can! I wanted to do that for him! You're the one who said no. Both of you did, so don't you dare put this at my feet."

The outburst made Ozzie jump. He watched his normally stoic godfather clamp a hand over his mouth, as if desperate to try and keep in everything else he wanted to say. The damage was done. Tears were already lining Ha-Yun's eyes, and Ethan looked so crushed by guilt that he could barely lift his head.

"Ozzie needs to go to Black River," Percival said at last. "The key is always hidden somewhere within the old Bell estate. The others will help him find it."

"The others? You mean the ones selected from the other families?" Ethan asked.

Percival nodded. Reaching across the kitchen island, he cupped a warm hand over Ozzie's arm. The touch was comforting, and Ozzie felt fearful tears start to burn the back of his eyes.

"Together we survive, alone we die. That is the only thing you can ever trust within the Witch Woods. They will be your strongest allies and surest weapons. She will do whatever she can to try and break that bond. You can't let her."

"What bond? I've never met these people."

"You should have." Percival spoke in a whisper, but his parents reeled as if they had been struck. "But the others will know about Katrina and you. You'll have to take a lot on faith and build these relationships as quickly as you can. I'll help you."

"How?" Ozzie asked.

Percival smiled slightly. "We can start by posting your selection."

"Posting?" Ethan asked.

There was warmth back in his voice as he casually revealed they had a website.

Chapter 6

Latching onto the chance to do something helpful, Ha-Yun rushed to retrieve her laptop. Within minutes, Percival was navigating his way to the website while the Davis family pushed tightly in around him.

Percival paused and lifted his head. "I'm not comfortable doing this with someone breathing down my neck."

"Put it up on the big screen?" Ethan suggested, remote already in hand.

A click of the button brought a plasma screen out of the wall. It almost consumed the space, and the group had only to turn around to view the details clearly. Ozzie had to admit it was far more comfortable. He could almost pretend he was just watching a movie play out. The soft tick of the box seemed to grow louder as if to mock him.

"This is the website?" Ethan asked when vibrant, cheerful colors filled the 103-inch screen.

Cute little cartoon characters bounded around the scattered links. Recipes, holiday reviews, fashion, and decorating tips. The place looked like a family run lifestyle page. A few clicks and a password brought them to a page simply marked 'The Harvest.' Below, the links were marked by the year concerned. They started in 1821. Ozzie's insides tightened a little more as Percival mindlessly scrolled down the list. Hearing this nightmare had been going on for nearly two centuries was one thing. It hadn't really had the same impact as seeing it laid out before him did. All the while, the box continued to scrape and click.

Finally, Percival selected a link and the screen changed again. Not to another variety of links—rather, a picture of a man filled the screen. He was unmistakably older than Ozzie, hovering somewhere between his twenties and thirties. Old enough that wrinkles had forged around his warm brown eyes. The light in the photograph made it hard to tell if he was graying or just had some really pale blonde streaks in his floppy brown hair. High cheekbones, a strong jawline, and a wide, thin mouth gave him an almost rattlesnake kind of smile.

"Oh, thank God." Percival slumped forward, rubbed a hand over his scalp, and pulled back with a jerk. "Thank God."

"Who is he?" Ethan asked.

Ha-Yun shook her head, "I don't know if I trust him or not."

"That's Cadwyn Winthrop. Cad if you get on his good side. And we're damn lucky he got selected."

Percival finished a gulp of wine before he continued, his tone shifting into something clinical and sterile. That tone, more than anything else, told Ozzie just how difficult what lay ahead was going to be.

"This is Cadwyn's first time being selected. His brother, however, was in a Harvest and lost. Inexplicably, Abraham made it out of the woods. You have to understand the demons don't just like to physically torment you. Their goal is to destroy you mentally as well. One of their favorite ways to do that is isolation. They turn themselves into such a threat that family members have no option but to take a step back." Tears loomed in the back of his throat, making his voice crackle.

He's done it before. The fact locked into Ozzie's mind, leaving only the question of how many times he had been forced to pick his own survival over the wellbeing of loved ones.

"Cadwyn's a living legend. He never left his brother's side until his death."

"He managed to be a decent human being," Ha-Yun said. "That's how low the bar is?"

Anger flashed through Percival's eyes but didn't make it out of his mouth.

"You saw the opening act for these creatures. Imagine enduring that every day for close to a year, only it can touch you. And all the while you know the one you're enduring this hell for is going to die. Or worse."

"What could be worse?" Ethan asked, dumbfounded.

Percival took another mouthful. "It's been documented on numerous occasions that, once the demon has weakened its target, it can take possession of the body. If this situation isn't corrected, the demon can then use the body to kill those outside of the family."

"Corrected?" Ethan asked. "You mean 'killed,' right? It forces you to kill each other."

"Is that what happened to Cadwyn and Abraham?" Ha-Yun asked.

Percival saluted them both with his wine glass. "I can't go into details."

"What?" Ha-Yun asked, too shocked to look enraged.

"You're neither blood nor bride," Percival shrugged. "There're some things that aren't spoken of outside of the family. What I can tell you is I know Cadwyn. He's loyal, protective, intelligent, and a registered psych nurse."

"You've also just suggested he may have murdered his brother," Ethan said in passing, leaping up to begin pacing the room.

"What you need to know from the story is this: at twelve years old, Cadwyn played chicken with a demon, and the demon blinked first." He turned to Ozzie to add, "If I could personally choose who would go into those woods with you, Cadwyn would be in my top ten. Play to his protective instincts. Build a friendship with him. If you can earn his loyalty, he'll die for you."

"I don't want to manipulate anyone," Ozzie said softly.

"Don't think of it as manipulation. Everyone else has had a lifetime to build these bonds, you're just playing catch-up." With that resolved, he scrolled down.

Ozzie perked up at the next photo to grace the screen. The girl was around his age, maybe a little older, with large dark eyes that matched her hair, tawny skin, a warm smile, and a figure that could stop traffic.

"She's cute."

"This isn't a dating site," Ethan mumbled, only to have his wife swiftly remind him their son wasn't blind.

During all of this, Percival had reached for one of the forgotten glasses. It was the most Ozzie had ever seen him drink. He had never known the old man could handle his liquor so well.

"That's Willimina Crane. Mina," he corrected with a shrug.

Ethan eyed his friend closely. "Is she going to be a problem?"

Percival snorted, "She isn't exactly an assist. See, she's one of the babies of the Crane line, and her folks insisted on treating her like it. They've kept her as far away from all of this as they could."

"So, she's in the same position as me?" Ozzie asked.

Percival shook his head as he continued to drink. "No. She knows her history. The problem is she doesn't believe it. For years, she's been trying to convince people this whole thing is a string of bad luck, natural gas leaks causing hallucinations, and group hysteria. Basically, she's a coddled little princess." He puffed out his chest and woefully clicked his tongue. "Katrina's going to have fun with her."

"What do you mean?" Ethan asked. "Surely, if her selection process was anything like Ozzie's, she now knows it's real."

"Katrina tends to treat skeptics one of two ways; either she crushes them under evidence until they're blabbering messes, or she makes sure to foster their doubt. The point is to take them out of the game. Have the Harvest fighting amongst themselves instead of working as a single-minded whole." Taking a sobering breath, he glanced at her photograph again. "No one wants to go in with a skeptic."

"Are you saying she's going to get Ozzie killed?" Ha-Yun asked.

Percival flinched. "Mina's weapon to wield is her tenaciousness. The girl's like a cassowary..."

"A what?" Ozzie cut in.

"It's a giant bird, okay?" Percival said. "A very large, very aggressive bird that uses five-inch-long claws to murder anything that annoys it. The point is, the girl's relentless. Once she sets her mind to something, you can't stop her. If she gets on board, she could be a remarkable ally. If she doesn't, well, the group will have to handle that."

Before anyone could question exactly what that would entail, he moved the page down again. No one in the Davis family seemed to know how to react to the last member of the group. Even without a size reference, it was clear the girl was tiny. In combination with porcelain skin, hair like spun gold, and delicate features, she'd easily be confused with a doll.

"She's a child," Ethan said at last.

It was then they noticed Percival's silence. His eyes spoke horror, but a smile played across his lips.

"There's no age limit," he muttered absently, as if the response was a knee-jerk reaction. "The oldest selected was ninety-two. The youngest was three weeks."

As the family reeled from all the thoughts and images that piece of information summoned, Percival let a quick burst of laughter pass his lips.

"Who is she?" Ozzie asked.

"That's Basheba Bell."

"Like the story?" Ethan cut in.

"Don't worry, she's not the same girl. That's just one of the weirder aspects of the curse. No matter our intentions, we always repeat the old family names."

"That's stupid," Ha-Yun muttered.

"Probably. What was it you wanted to call your son again?"

"Park." Ha-Yun's eyes stretched wide, her jaw dropping as if it had just occurred to her that she never had any intention of naming her child Osgood.

Deciding his point had been proven, Percival saluted the image with a glass. "You know that top ten list I mentioned? Basheba would be in my top five."

Ozzie studied the photograph again, trying to see what Percival could possibly be talking about. There was a doe-eyed naivety about her. No matter how long he looked, Basheba seemed like the kind of girl who would be utterly mystified by bubbles.

"I give up," Ozzie said. "What's so special about her?"

"Most notably, this isn't her first rodeo," Percival said. "She was selected for Harvest two years ago."

"Is that allowed?" Ethan asked.

"The Bell family has dwindled over the years. The smaller the bloodline, the higher the likelihood of getting selected. There's only four of them left. No, sorry. Three." Percival's eyes clouded over as he made the correction. "There's three, now. Jonathan didn't make it out last year."

While his grief was never spoken, it still filled the room and made the air thick. No one disturbed Percival as his body stilled. For a brief moment, the man's eyes closed and a fine tremor raced over his shoulders. Ozzie was sure he was about to cry. But then, with a sharp intake of breath through his nose, he returned to his cool demeanor.

"Basheba knows first-hand what ya'll are walking into. Yeah, she's small and not much of a physical help. But she's quick on her feet, ruthless, and practical. She'll be willing to cut Mina loose if she's not going to pull her weight."

"Isn't that going against the group unity you keep talking about?" Ethan asked.

"Sometimes, you have to give up a lamb to save the flock."

The way Percival greedily shot the last of the wine like it was whiskey left Ozzie convinced that this, too, was something the older man had personal experience with.

"She's a good kid," Percival said at last. "But the last few years have left their mark. We'll have to be careful to win her over before you head out."

"What do you mean by that?" Ha-Yun asked.

He gestured out like the response was obvious. "Which one of them do you think is going to be excited by the prospect of going into the Witch Woods with a complete novice? No one wants to be stuck babysitting while fighting for their lives. We have to ensure none of them think of Ozzie as dead weight. Cadwyn's proven he's capable of mercy killings, Mina's nothing if not practical, and Basheba's seen too much to be kindhearted." He chuckled slightly. "This is the one time where being unpopular could actually get you killed."

Ethan nodded, his motion calm while his eyes blazed with panic. "What do you suggest we do?"

"First of all, we have to make sure we get there first." Not leaving any room for argument, Percival got to his feet, hurriedly swallowing down the last of the red liquid. "Each selected has exactly seven days from when the box is handed to them, so time is a factor. Dragging your feet with getting to Black River is an unforgivable crime. If we take a helicopter, we can make it there in about an hour and forty minutes. Traditionally, if we have the time, the selected spend a day setting out a strategy and getting a good night's sleep. Ozzie, you'll be picking up the tab for all of it. Everything. Without question. We Sewalls are still the best off financially, and we're going to remind them of our generosity. Understood?"

"Yeah." Ozzie cleared his throat and spoke again with something he hoped sounded like conviction. "Yes, let's do this."

"That's the spirit. Grab the box and let's go."

Ozzie hesitated. The box still sat on the middle of the kitchen counter, shining in the overhead lights. Popping and scraping as the pieces moved. He jumped when Percival placed a warm hand on his shoulder.

"No matter what happens, you can't lose that box," he said gravely. "Your survival depends on it. Pick it up now, and don't let it leave your person until this is done."

Ozzie nodded. *I can do this. She's a dead witch. I'm a Davis. A Sewall. There's nothing that can get the better of me.*

For all his conviction, the box still lay there, untouched.

Chapter 7

Time didn't work the same in Black River as it did everywhere else. Nested within miles of untouched wilderness, the farming town seemed content with the simpler way of life. Plentiful crops of corn and wheat saw them through the summer. The winter harvest stood ready for the picking. Stalks with bulbous puffs of cotton, fields of plump pumpkins, and orchards full of crimson apples spread out over the undulating earth. The woods rose up sharply at the edges of the outlying properties. Towering old growths of oak and maple worked together to enclose the town.

The autumn night hung over the area, thick with chill and still as the grave. Basheba knew the instant she entered the town limits. Not by some shift in the forest or the sudden emergence of the crops. It was the moonlight. From Nashville, it had hung low in the sky, drenching the calm world with silver light. The moment she entered Black River, it died away, wilting until there was barely a trace of it left to touch the road before her.

Buck hadn't lifted his head from the crook of Basheba's arm. He had dozed on and off for the forty-five-minute drive, only stirring to growl softly at the glove box. She didn't try to move the object. Simply kept her focus locked onto the dark road as she weaved past the ancient homesteads. Her grip on the wheel tightened when she approached the last obstacle that properly separated the town from the surrounding farmlands.

There were numerous points where the river that gave the town its name thinned into little more than a babbling brook. Naturally, it was at these markers the first settlers had decided to construct bridges, and the town hadn't seen any reason to change that. Most of them hadn't even been upgraded and remained as little more than a few planks hastily nailed together. There were a couple that had been changed into covered bridges. She had purposefully gone a mile out of her way to ensure she managed to cross at one of these points.

A dull overhanging light bulb illuminated the opening and she set her gaze upon it, breathed deep and slow, locked her elbows, and pushed down the accelerator.

The car lurched forward over the gravel road. Her headlights flooded the elongated cave of the tunneled bridge and washed over the dark water. A broken cry escaped Basheba as she put her entire body weight down on the brake. The tires locked and skidded over the loose earth. With a final lurch that threw her against her seatbelt and sent Buck tumbling onto the cab floor, the car came to a halt.

"Sorry, sorry," Basheba whispered as Buck scrambled his way back up.

It took a concerted effort to loosen her death grip on the wheel. She gave him an apology scratch behind his ears.

"Sorry," she breathed one last time.

Don't look. Just don't look. It was impossible to listen to her own advice. The dark water drew her gaze. It shifted like liquid onyx around the stones that stood out like exposed bones. Her heart hammered painfully against her ribs, each beat rattling her small frame.

"It's only a few inches deep," she told Buck. "Only a few inches."

He grumbled, nose twitching wildly as he glanced around. Watching his fruitless efforts to find the source of her anxiety made her feel like an idiot. She gave him another scratch.

"I'm okay. You're with me, right boy?"

Buck plopped his butt down on the seat, straightening his front legs, a guard dog at its post. At least, that's what she liked to think of him as.

"All right. We're going to just shoot on through. It'll only take a second."

Not trusting herself to see through her conviction on the first attempt, she ordered the Rottweiler onto the floor in front of the passenger seat. Once he was safely stowed away, she put her manual car in gear, took a deep breath, and stomped down. She was forced to shift rapidly as the car picked up speed. Flimsy wooden walls kept the river from her view. Basheba locked her eyes on the end of the tunnel, racing toward it, the process only taking a few seconds.

A sudden jerk threw her forward. Her seatbelt tensed, crushing the air from her lungs before forcing her back. Buck yelped, the headlights died, and the roar of the engine was reduced to a hollow rapid clicking. Wincing, Basheba struggled to understand what had just happened.

Vaguely, she was aware that the abrupt stop had sloshed her brain around her skull. *Whiplash?* The thought was quickly dismissed. All the pain in her body existed in the single bar where her seatbelt had struck her.

"Buck, you okay, boy?"

Deprived of both high beams and moonlight, shadows strangled the world around her. Buck's fur was the perfect camouflage. She groped for the seatbelt, calling for him again when she first heard it. Something moving within the water. The door muted the sound but she recognized it instantly. Snapping into motion, she hunched forward, slipping her emergency bag out from under her seat. Leaning to the side, she blindly fumbled with the latch of the glove box. The instant she had the witch's music box in hand, she thrust open the passenger door and rolled out, calling for Buck to follow. A bark and scrape of claws indicated he was following.

Don't look back. Don't stop. The self-commands unbidden and unnecessary. Past experience had already sent a surge of adrenaline through her veins. Cold air burned her lungs as she sprinted for the far end of the bridge. The wooden slats rattled under her feet. Small gaps opened to allow the sound of rushing water to echo around her.

The unseen presence consumed the distance between them, slithering through the water with impossible speed. Water exploded through the slats like a geyser, drenching her as the scent of damp earth and decaying moss spewed into the air.

Buck yelped and snarled. Basheba gathered her strength and leaped forward. Still air struck her as she broke free of the wall of water. With a sharp twist, she managed to land hard on her shoulder and duck into a bone-rattling but effective roll. She came to a stop on all fours, snapping back around to stare at the bridge, fingers clutching both her bag and the music box.

Whatever force that had kept the water rising died with a low hiss. Gravity took hold, bringing the droplets back down like a pattering rain.

Panting hard, Basheba scanned the lonesome road, absentmindedly patting Buck when he ran forward to lick the river water off of her cheek. A few unseen night birds chirped from the treetops. The stream gurgled lazily against the stones. Buck's nails scratched shallow grooves into the dirt as he bumped and wiggled for her attention.

Basheba never stopped scanning the river as she crammed the enchanted cube into her backpack. Still refusing to look down, she patted the slick, waterproof material repeatedly, searching for the trademark shape. Only then did she rise to her feet.

A shift in the water instantly drew her attention. The dull moonlight caught the minuscule breaking waves more than the object that had disrupted the flow did. Her attention locked onto the curved blob, narrowing her focus until it was the only thing she could see.

Suddenly, twin orbs broke through the pitch darkness of the object. Eyes. Impossibly wide, burning red, and fixated on her. There wasn't time to process the sight before light shattered the darkness, rendering her blind.

Her car's engine roared like a wounded animal. The feeble planks of the bridge strained under the rapidly moving vehicle. Regaining all of its previously lost momentum, the car barreled toward her. She spun on her heel, calling for Buck to follow her as she sprinted away from the approaching high beams.

Gravel crunched and the engine whined behind her. Basheba lunged desperately for the tree line. Her feet got tangled and she dropped like a stone. Thorny bushes slashed at her as she dropped down behind them. A colossal cracking thud sounded before chipped bark sprayed over her back like shrapnel. She scrambled forward, ignoring the spikes of pain as she sought shelter. A nearby thunderous crack made her freeze.

She shivered in the resulting silence. Every ounce of pain she had ignored made itself known, leaving her breathless and whimpering as she freed herself from the tangled mass of spikes.

The night was dark once more. Scrambling, she pulled her phone from her pocket. A cobweb of fine cracks distorted the lock screen picture but the flashlight app still worked.

"Buck?" The first call was barely more than a whisper. But when she received no reply, it rose to a shout. "Buck!"

Basheba knew she was projecting when she decided his bark sounded relieved. The Rottweiler bound into the glow of her phone.

"Good boy," she gushed while fighting her way back onto the road. "Smart boy."

He reared up as she approached, balancing his front paws on her shoulders to better lick her face. She almost buckled under the extra weight.

"Are you okay, Buck? Did she hurt you?"

Logically, she knew he couldn't answer. So she rubbed his flank encouragingly while shoving him into motion. About half a yard down the road, her car was now wrapped around the thick trunk of a tree. Glass scattered across the ground, shining like diamonds in the flickering headlights. A thin string of steam curled up from the now dead engine with a serpentine hiss.

Basheba eyed the tree as she closed in on the totaled vehicle. "A witch elm? Really, Kat? It's a little on the nose, don't you think?"

Yelling into the darkness only made her feel better for a moment. After that, the gnawing dread ravaging her stomach forced her into action. She checked for the box once more, slipped her backpack on, and headed down the road in a lurching jog.

***

Cadwyn eased up on the brakes and pulled his motorcycle into the gas station. The 2016 Triumph Thruxton's primal growl echoed over the open slab of concrete. In anticipation of the Harvest, he had slept as much as he could. It didn't really matter, though. Stonebridge and Black River were separated by a seventeen-hour drive. With a full shift on top of that, there was no way to avoid the effects of sleep deprivation. He clung to the hope that the others arrived promptly, allowing them the luxury of a full night's sleep in a proper bed.

The leather of his riding gear crackled as he swung a long leg off the bike. He stumbled. The extended ride had turned his muscles into stone. Pain sparked under the waves of pins and needles that covered his skin.

Cadwyn swallowed a few curse words and carefully stretched out his legs, his back, his arms. *Caffeine.* The reminder made him turn toward the door. Halfway there, he recalled he also needed to fill up his Thruxton. At least the extra pacing helped to work the blood flow back into his legs.

That done, he retraced his steps back to the gas station, ignoring the few people who were watching him. The dawn was pushing against the horizon, giving the gas station a thin but steady flow of early risers on their way out and people just coming off of night shifts.

He remembered entering the doors. Then everything was covered in a fog, clearing after he had been staring at the drinks fridge for who knew how long. It would put his organs through hell, but he gathered up a half dozen energy drinks, the kind loaded with enough caffeine to put an elephant into cardiac arrest. Cadwyn guzzled down one of the cans as he made his way to the counter.

"Hey," the bored clerk said.

Cadwyn forced a smile in greeting and held up the can he was working on to make sure they added it to his bill. The others, he dumped on the counter.

"Pump five, thanks."

"Long night?" The clerk chuckled.

"It's going to be a long week," he replied, glancing up as he started to count out a couple of bills.

A looming abyss reared up behind the man, a dark shadow the overhead lights couldn't touch. It was thick and wide and lunging toward Cadwyn. He jumped back, knocking over a display and scattering candy bars across the floor.

"Hey!"

In the space of a blink, the shadow dissolved, leaving only a confused minimum wage employee.

"Are you all right?"

"Yes." Cadwyn rubbed a hand over his face, digging his knuckles into his eyes. "I'm fine. Thanks. Sorry."

He had just begun to gather up the bars when the clerk came around and helped him.

"It's okay, I've got it."

"I'm really sorry," Cadwyn said.

The clerk took the bars and studied Cadwyn carefully. "Are you okay to drive?"

He nodded rapidly and got to his feet, making sure to leave the change as an apology tip. Another of the energy drinks was gone by the time he had returned to his bike. He could feel it strumming through him like a live wire. It still wasn't enough to drive the dry, aching feeling from his eyes. A few swift smacks and the cool air helped a little.

Call someone. The thought seemed to come from a distant echo chamber. It took a few seconds for him to realize what his own mind was telling him. The Bluetooth in his helmet would allow him to keep a conversation going. The question was who he would call. His clouded mind dredged up the answer that left him cold. *Rudolph.*

Crushed under a wave of guilt and grief, he didn't notice the first patters against the high metal awning. It was only when it picked up speed and became a downpour of hail that he paid it any attention. A moment later, his brain caught up with why.

It doesn't sound right.

A lighter tinkle. A different pattern. The morning sun drove back the shadows, illuminating the tiny objects falling from the sky.

His stomach clenched, almost forced the sugary drink back up his throat. Clamping a hand over his mouth, he swallowed rapidly and fixed his eyes on the ground. Soon enough, the constant stream of falling teeth bounced into his field of vision, their jagged ends encrusted with withered flesh and stained with blood.

She's trying to stop you. They're not real.

Knowing that didn't make it any easier. After stowing away the drinks, he shoved his helmet on. Teeth scattered around his feet as he threw a leg over his bike.

Through the tinted visor, he caught sight of the downpour once more. Fine tremors shook his hands, remaining even while he twisted his grip around the handles. His stomach rolled, sloshing the minimal contents of his stomach and threatening to bring it back up.

Falling teeth caught on the wind, swirling as they fell until they completely covered the ground. Cadwyn squeezed his eyes closed to block it out. Before he could calm his rapid heartbeat, sleep reared up within him, and he was forced to open them again. Forced to watch the unnatural rain, to hear the tiny patter as they skittered across the ground.

He gagged.

You have to go. You have to keep moving. You're running late.

The motivation gave him enough strength to stomp down and bring his bike roaring to life. The familiar sound covered the worst of the noise, but there was still the sight to deal with. *It's just hail.*

Instead of the phone call, he turned on his music, pushing up the volume until he couldn't hear the teeth crunch under the wheels of his bike. Clenching his jaw until it ached and unable to quell the tremors that racked his body, he peeled out. *Just get to Black River.*

Chapter 8

Ozzie couldn't get over the fact that the whole forest looked like it was on fire. He'd seen autumn leaves before, but nothing like this. Endless shades of red and yellow stained the foliage. They blazed in the morning light and shimmered with the slightest breeze. It was hypnotic, and he found himself staring unblinkingly for moments on end. *The lack of sleep probably isn't helping,* he thought, blinking rapidly to remoisten his dry eyes.

Being forced to wait for the rest of the world to wake up had been its own kind of torment. Logically, they knew the wait was worth it. Chartering a helicopter would get them to Tennessee faster than taking a standard flight or driving. But knowing that didn't make the wait any easier. Ozzie's parents had paced endlessly across the gravel entrance to the airfield, literally creating a trench. It was small and mostly consisted of high heel marks, but Ozzie had decided it counted.

Percival had tried to keep them all distracted, regaling them with stories of past Harvests and all those who had survived. While Ozzie had done his best to listen, his attention had always been drawn back to the box. It had shone like molten gold in the first few rays of daybreak. Every now and then, he was sure he could feel something moving inside of it.

Stifling a yawn, Ozzie scrubbed a hand through his thick black hair and leaned against the window. *It's actually kind of pretty,* he thought as he watched the scorching colors pass by. He had thought, once he had the moment to think, he could do just that—explore his deepest soul and bring the chaos of his mind into a coherent order once again. It just seemed like something he should be doing.

It hadn't worked out that way.

He had tried to think, put the full force of his mind and determination into it, about what was waiting for him. He tried to think of different ways he could win the others over, or even about all the things that had forever changed now that he knew all that paranormal stuff was real. But he couldn't keep his mind from straying. A few times, he had taken a run at the easiest topic before him.

How do I feel about being a Sewall?

He adored his family; loved his life in general. Only a few hours ago he had learned it was all a lie.

Not to mention my godfather is genetically my dad.

It felt weird to even think of it. All his life, his mother and Percival had been like siblings. Emotionally close, sporadically annoying each other, and with zero romantic tension. It was just gross to think they had been together like that, let alone produced him.

And no one cared! At least, not enough to let me know.

That was about the limits of his organized thought process. Over and over, his brain crumbled the moment he reached that point. He tried to grasp the thoughts, force himself to lead them to their inevitable conclusion, but never could. Everything always brought him back to the same point.

The image of Maxwell with spiders burrowing out of his flesh.

Not Maxwell, he told himself. *It just made itself look like him. Maxwell is fine. Spiders don't do that.*

Images of twisting, hairy spider legs flashed across his mind. Bile burnt the back of his throat as his stomach roiled. The helicopter rotated at the same moment. Sunlight found the box again, glinting off it to create a blinding glare that jerked him from his spiraling thoughts.

Instinctively, his fingers tightened around the box until his bones hurt. He began to slowly twist the cube back and forth, letting the sunlight dance off the polished sides. His brow furrowed when he noticed that the constantly moving puzzle pieces never pinched his fingers. A small quiver rattled the innards.

Was the demon I saw the same as what's trapped inside this thing?

Ice entered his stomach as another question tore its way into the forefront of his mind. *It's 'trapped,' but it can do that. What else can it do?*

What scared him was the possibility that, at some point, it could have all been real. Physically real. That he could have touched that grotesque sight. *That it could have touched me.* With a visible flinch, he forced his gaze back to the sea of foliage, desperate for some distraction.

There's so much of it. The woods stretched out to the horizon in every direction. A thick blanket disrupted only by the deep grooves left by passing streams. Without warning, the dense trees gave way to farmlands. Fields of crops and cattle zipped by within an instant, and they were left hovering over the small township of Black River.

The thick stream the place was named after divided the town in two. Even from above, the conscious effort to keep the town's rustic aesthetic was evident. The few undeniably modern buildings scattered about tried their best to camouflage themselves amongst the antique architecture. An old chapel still held the place of pride atop the only distinctive hill in the area. Made of black wood and spearing the sky with a single steeple, it was the largest building in the whole town.

Ozzie's pilot had to circle the area twice before he found the small patch of land subbing for an airport. Black River didn't have a real airport. What they had was the local sporting ground that hadn't had anything else going on that day, and was grateful for the large donation. Lush green and well-tended, the short grass whipped violently as they landed. With Percival settling things with the landowners, and his parents handling the final matters with the pilot, there was nothing for Ozzie to do but get out and study the alien surroundings.

Black River wasn't like anything he had ever seen. While his parents liked to travel, it had always been to places like Italy, Rome, Las Vegas, or the Bahamas. Places designed to meet their needs and entertain them with an endless array of wonders. This place, while having a quaint charm, was about as far away from his norm as he could imagine. It left him feeling both larger than life and insignificantly tiny at the same time.

With a sudden rush of clarity, Ozzie realized he was completely out of his depth.

I have no idea what I'm doing. I've never even been camping! They're all going to know I'm useless. I'm going to get everyone killed.

Ozzie turned, instinct demanding he get back onto the helicopter and get out. A lump of pure dread crystalized in his stomach as he was left to watch the helicopter rise into the clear sky.

"Where's the car?" Ethan asked over the sound of the chopper's blades, then caught sight of his son.

Concern wrinkled his brow as he studied Ozzie's face. He didn't say anything, though, just placed a hand on his son's shoulder and gave it a reassuring squeeze.

The harsh wind died and the retreating engine left them to the mercy of the early morning silence that lingered over the town. Time seemed to hover, broken only by a breath of wind that made the distant leaves whisper. Ozzie shivered and inched closer to his father.

Percival stalked over, casually adjusting his overcoat. "What was that?"

"The car?" Ha-Yun prompted.

"I didn't hire one," Percival replied. Noticing the looks of his companions, he added, "Black River doesn't have the infrastructure to handle the influx of the four families. Not to mention the tourist season. It's just quicker to walk."

Ozzie hurried to fall in step alongside the much taller man. *Can't wait for my dang growth spurt.* The passing thought caught him off guard. It was strange to think that, even while his brain was breaking under the weight of the new information, there was still enough room left for his regular self to slip through. In a strange way, he found it rather comforting. It was a small bit of normalcy that he desperately clung to.

"This place has a tourist season?" Ozzie asked.

The short look Percival threw him made him stammer.

"I'm not saying your hometown isn't pretty. It's nice. I'm sure there's a crowd who would love to come out this way. I hear a lot of people like to travel to see the leaves change color. I mean, that's," he paused as he winced. *We've talked about this Ozzie. If you don't know how you're going to end a sentence, don't start it.* "A thing," he stammered.

Percival's tense expression was softened by a smile he fought to smother. "I wasn't born here, Oz. Even if I was, I'd still hate this place."

"Oh. Then, what's up with..." Again, he didn't have a way to end it, so he swirled a finger out to indicate Percival's vanishing smile.

"As a Sewall, it's our duty to hate the tourist trade here."

"Why?"

"No one's coming here to see the autumn aesthetics, Ozzie."

It still wasn't clicking in Ozzie's head, and he glanced back to his father for some help. Ethan fell into step on Percival's other side and asked the question.

"Then what's the real reason?"

Percival kept his gaze locked straight ahead. "The Witch."

Ozzie longed to be able to meet his parent's eyes and see if they were just as confused as he was. Unfortunately, he also didn't want to be so obvious about it as to jog forward and peer around his godfather, so he was stuck doing nothing but shifting his fingers over the box.

"People come to see Katrina?" Ha-Yun asked.

Percival paused mid-stride. Instantly, he had everyone's unwavering attention.

"Don't call her by name. Not around here."

Ha-Yun's eyes widened and she leaned closer to whisper, "Does it heighten her powers?"

"No," he snorted. "She's essentially a serial killer who's specifically preyed on our families for close to two centuries. Hearing her name, well, for the people you're about to meet, it'll be like moseying into

Waterloo and bringing up John Wayne Gacy."

"But she's a tourist attraction?" Ethan asked.

"Her legend is," he replied, evidently bitter. He started walking again. "In and of itself, her life wasn't much to write home about. The whole world is full of psychopaths systematically ruining random people's lives. After death, however, The Bell Witch became one of the most documented cases of poltergeist activity in the world. To this day, there's barely a case that measures up to the number of eyewitness accounts, collected evidence, and spirit photography."

"They had cameras back then?" Ozzie asked.

Percival was so caught off guard by the question that he forgot to cover his laugh.

"What? No, they didn't. But people came out here after cameras were invented. They *still* come out here. I–" He choked on his own words and shook his head. "How is this confusing you?"

Ozzie shrugged, keeping his mouth shut. Eventually, Percival went back to what he had been saying.

"She's also a witch. Some folks are into that kind of thing. That interest has allowed Black River to build a tourism industry somewhat like Salem. Or the Amityville Horror house, depending on who you talk to. Some come for the tragic history while others just want to see a ghost."

It didn't take long for the group to be confronted with numerous examples of what Percival was talking about. Halloween had invaded the town. Old fashioned decorations clustered around the buildings and lined the streets. None of them were the flashy, plastic things Ozzie was used to. Draped sheets fluttered in the crisp morning air, looking like formless ghosts. Scarecrows released small creaks and groans as they swayed on their spikes. The bulbous sides of fat Jack 'o' lanterns distorted their frozen grins into sinister smirks. But it was the witches amongst them that sent stray shivers down Ozzie's spine. They clung to the lampposts, filled the windows, and dangled from the skeletal arms of the trees.

Ozzie protectively cradled the box to his stomach as they continued down the street. The further they went, the more evidence he found of the town embracing their home-grown urban legend.

It seemed every street corner had a folding board advertising a different ghost tour or Witch Wood's hike. Most of the businesses they passed were a play on puns or direct references, most notably the distant café called Witch's Brew. The lampposts had originally been fashioned to look like the old gas burning kind. At some point, someone must have suggested that changing their tops into pointed black witch hats would be hilarious. Even the town's library had a few cackling, black hatted crones pushed up on their windows.

Black River wasn't a town that opened up their Main Street early. Most of the businesses remained closed and dark as they made a beeline to the Witch's Brew. The welcome sign was still switched to 'closed,' but the door wasn't locked, and Percival didn't hesitate to push his way through.

Nighttime shadows lingered within the café. Chairs were stacked upon the rounded tables and, every now and then, Ozzie caught the sterile scent of floor cleaner. A small silver bell affixed above the door announced their arrival. It didn't take more than that soft tinkle to have the unseen back doors slam open.

An instant later, the swinging door behind the counter opened to unleash a flood of people. Their chatter filled the space like an approaching storm. In seconds, they were surrounded. Everyone was talking at once. Introductions came hard and fast until Ozzie couldn't recall a single person. All he knew was they were all Sewalls. *My relatives.* It was overwhelming. Crammed into this room alone were more relatives than he had ever had with both of his parent's families combined.

Swept up in the retreating tide, they were ushered around the corner and out the back door. Working together in a whirlwind of limbs and well wishes, they bundled him through the kitchen and out the back door. Somewhere along the line, he was handed a glass of lemonade and a plate piled high with chicken fresh off the grill.

The sudden shift in both mood and location left Ozzie stunned. He found himself constantly looking back over his shoulder to make sure he hadn't been transported somewhere.

We were just on Mainstreet.

He was sure of that. And the building itself wasn't too large. Crossing its innards wouldn't have brought them back out to the woods. It seemed he was standing in someone's rural backyard.

It was spacious, with the curve of the road behind them mirroring the bend in the river. A flat patch of earth separated the back of the building from the riverbed, with enough room to comfortably fit a bonfire and numerous large tables. Strings of lights hung in scalloped rows from tree branches that were heavy with bright foliage. They dangled loosely, offering a rather useless glow that couldn't compete with the early morning sunlight.

There were more leaves on the ground than trees to account for them. They created a thick and squishy mulch blanket.

The Black River lived up to its name even while drenched in sunlight. It was impossible to judge its depth. Here and there, the glassy surface broke against a stone, giving the appearance the stream couldn't be more than a few inches deep. At other points, the still, dark waters seemed bottomless. It lay like a sheet of polished oil stretching out for about thirty feet before giving way to the woods. A heavy stone, covered in orange moss and evergreens, jutted out toward them from the far side. Ozzie hated the sight of it.

The people who had welcomed them soon bled into the swirling crowd. It looked as if they had just walked in on a celebration. Tired but happy faces. Drinks still flowing from the night before.

Ozzie clutched his music box tight, jabbing it against his stomach and twisting his wrists into painful angles in an attempt to cover it as much as possible.

Was this all a prank?

Before him was an ocean of happy faces. Laughter and the scent of barbeque hung heavy in the air while children ran about in giggling swarms. Confronted with all of this, it was hard to think it was anything but a sick joke. Ozzie desperately tried to pinpoint which of his more ridiculous but organized friends could pull something like this off.

"What is this?" Ethan demanded, his voice sharp but his volume low.

"This is my family. I told you they'd all be here waiting."

"They're having a party?" Ha-Yun asked.

Percival tipped his head to the side. He seemed to find that more dignified than a shrug. "Wouldn't you?"

"If everything you've told us is true," she stressed, "then all of these people know someone could die."

"And they know, at least this year, it's not them."

Ethan stammered. "So they celebrate? That's sick."

"What would you have us do? Ensure the last few hours the Selected gets to spend with their family is full of dread and tears? To send them off into hell with the knowledge that no one expects them to return? That's sick, my friend. We make sure they have a few more happy memories to cling to when things get bad. This isn't supposed to be a funeral. It's a celebration of life and displaying absolute confidence the Selected will make it through."

"Still." Ha-Yun shivered and inched closer to Ozzie. "Don't you see this as a little twisted?"

No one had expected Percival to laugh at that. "My family has had this curse hanging over them for generations. And we're still here. Broken. Defiant. Flourishing. And sane. A huge part of the reason for that is that we embrace life. We celebrate it. Especially when things are bad."

Ha-Yun opened her mouth, but Percival quickly cut her off.

"When your family has been cursed for centuries, you can decide how you handle it. This is a Sewall matter. And you're not a Sewall."

A delighted squeal announced the arrival of a woman an instant before she threw herself into Percival's arms. After a tight hug, the questions started to flow, quick and random. She barely had confirmation this was, in fact, 'the' Osgood before she was asking about kitchen renovations and the state of affairs in Washington. Every so often, she would bounce back to Ozzie. But she never lingered. The moment her straying eyes fell upon the cube Ozzie kept tightly gripped in his arms, she would jerk away and force a smile.

"Don't take it personally," Percival whispered to him as the woman retreated, checking once again to make sure they weren't following her. "Some find it harder than others to deal with the reminders."

Ozzie swallowed thickly. Everything he wanted to say got trapped in his throat when he noticed the pain that quickly crossed his godfather's face.

"So, the hair loss situation is a family thing, huh?" Ozzie asked with as much playfulness as he could muster.

A loud bark of laughter escaped the older man. Ozzie wasn't ready for the pat on the back Percival gave him and lurched forward with the contact.

"Sorry. It's in the genetics."

"Great."

"Hey, a lot of people think it looks dignified."

Ozzie had just straightened himself again when another person knocked him from behind. This time, the box almost slipped from his hands. His heart lurched as he struggled to keep his fingers around the smooth surface.

"Basheba, sweetie, aren't you still underage?"

Ozzie jerked straight again. The speaker held no interest for him. Every ounce of attention he was capable of latched instantly onto the girl in front of him. Having pushed past him, Basheba had intercepted the beer an older man had brought for Percival. Condensation trickled from the beer bottle to clean thin trails on her mud-streaked skin. She didn't pause in guzzling down the amber liquid, only lifting one finger to keep the questioning man at bay for a little while. It allowed Ozzie a few moments to try to get his thoughts in line. Despite his effort, the first thing that popped into his head was, *she's tiny.*

She was at least a foot shorter than him. Her face had grown a little plumper than it had been in the photograph, and her legs were a little too long to be called stocky. The flannel shirt she wore was basically a dress. It hung limply over the miniscule frame, torn, muddy, and stained with blood. Leaves clung to the knot of hair bundled on the crown of her head. The layer of dirt wasn't enough to dull the golden sheen, though. Only after she had swallowed the last drop did she suck in a deep breath and address the man.

"Why, yes, Lucius, I am," she said, her voice as sweet as honeysuckle. "Do you have another?"

"I don't think your uncle would like that," Lucius replied.

Basheba smiled. A pretty expression on a pretty little face. But there wasn't even a hint of warmth to it.

"And, of course, his happiness is the sole focus of my existence."

Lucius opened his mouth, closed it, and turned to Percival for help. A single nod was all it took to send the man scurrying back toward the picnic tables. Basheba watched him go, her expression unchanging but ice forming within her gaze.

"How are you, Basheba?" Percival asked it like it was completely natural for her to show up in such a state.

Apparently, that was the correct move, because her mood instantly shifted. She looked like the living embodiment of a spring day as she said, "The Witch is a bitch."

Percival snapped his fingers. "I've had my suspicions for years."

"She totaled my car."

"Horrible woman. Are you injured?"

Basheba's lower jaw jutted out to the side as she suppressed her brewing rage. "I'm this close to going around town burning everything Katrina-related."

Percival flinched at the name but held his tongue. With that, Ozzie had reached his limit. It was all too much to suppress simultaneously.

"Why do *you* get to say her name?" he blurted out.

Basheba took a moment to look him over from head to toe before answering. "Who's going to stop me?"

"I just mean, well, Percival said it was like mentioning a serial killer to their victims."

He wasn't prepared for Basheba to roll her eyes and mutter about how she wanted another drink. It had never taken so little to make him feel like a complete idiot.

Pursing her lips, she let out a sharp whistle. The answering bark was instantaneous. The actual appearance of the dog took a little longer and was preceded with startled squeals and breaks in the crowd. Ozzie didn't understand until he saw the animal for himself.

The Rottweiler was massive. A hundred and twenty pounds of muscle and fangs. It circled around Basheba to tap its nose against her left hand. From paw to shoulder, the dog had to be two feet tall, at least. Straightening its front legs, it dumped its rump onto the mushy leaves and stared at her with unwavering intensity. Side by side with her pet, Basheba looked as breakable as glass.

"That's a big dog." Ethan struggled to sound casual while simultaneously attempting to gather his family closer to him. "I assume he's well trained?"

Both Basheba and the Rottweiler ignored him. She jerked a chin toward one of the ice buckets.

"Fetch."

The dog's lower fangs shone like polished marble before it was suddenly sprinting across the field, massive paws kicking up mud and leaves. That done, she returned her attention to the group before them.

"Quick question; who the hell are you?"

"Oh, um," Ozzie glanced helplessly to Percival. "You didn't check the website?"

"I was a little busy avoiding vehicular homicide. You might remember me mentioning that."

Ozzie blinked at her, "You were serious?"

It seemed like she wanted to glare at him, but her angelic face didn't allow for such an expression. It ended up as more of a pout, which Ozzie found unsettling.

How am I supposed to get a good read on her if she can't express things properly?

It was like playing poker with someone who had just left a Botox party.

Ozzie shuffled his feet and fought the urge to look at Percival again. *I can handle a conversation on my own. I can make her like me.*

"I just thought the witch couldn't do anything physical until–"

"Oh, you're Osgood." She said it as if the mystery had really been bothering her.

"Ozzie," he corrected with a shrug, only to be ignored.

Her attention was stolen by the immense black dog's return. One side of its lips was bunched up around the beer bottle it carried. Without prompting, it dropped the bottle into Basheba's waiting hand and graciously accepted a neck rub as reward.

"Good boy," she cooed as she read the label.

The animal melted into the touch, plastering itself to her side and looking up at her with utter adoration.

"Very good boy." Twisting open the top, she smirked at Percival. "He's even learned my brand."

Ha-Yun's motherly instinct couldn't be denied. "You mentioned earlier you were underage."

"I'm twenty," Basheba said slowly.

"Still," Ha-Yun pressed gently. "That's not twenty-one."

The blonde couldn't contain her giggle. "You're new here, aren't you?"

"Ha-Yun." Percival cleared his throat, seemingly sharing Basheba's amusement. "By now, you must realize being a member of the four families comes with a certain degree of stress. Everyone here has developed a tactic for dealing with it. Admittedly, some are healthier than others, but it's considered polite not to draw attention to them. Let alone criticize."

"So, you just ignore illegal activity that could be damaging her developing brain?" Ha-Yun turned back to Basheba. "What does your mother say about this?"

The younger woman stopped nursing the bottle to mumble around a full mouth, "Katrina killed her five years ago."

Ha-Yun instantly deflated. "Oh. I'm—"

"And I might die tomorrow," Basheba chirped.

In that moment, Ozzie found the small pixie of a woman incredibly creepy. It was in the smile. The brilliant, pristine smile matched with dead eyes.

Like a shark sensing blood, Basheba continued, her pleasant smile frozen in place.

"I'm for sure going to be tortured, both mentally and physically. Katrina might even let me see my father's death. She showed me my mother's two years ago. And brother's. Both my sisters'. Countless cousins. At this point, it'll be kind of mean not to let me know if my daddy died screaming or not. Like ruining a set."

Slowly, deliberately, she rose the bottle back to her lips. The tendrils of hair that hung around her face began to sway. It was the only hint she was trembling.

"I'm sorry." She tipped the bottle. "Does this bother you?"

"No," Ha-Yun said softly. She didn't appear to know what she wanted to express, and her face restlessly shifted through countless emotions. "No, it doesn't. I'm so sorry."

"Don't worry. I'll pace myself." She turned fully to Percival. "Where's Cadwyn?"

"He hasn't arrived yet."

"So, um," Ozzie lurched into the conversation, desperate to find a way to claw onto a better standing point with her. "Do you prefer BeBe?"

"What?"

"You know, Basheba Bell. BeBe. Or do you just go by your last name?"

"I prefer Basheba."

"Really?" He snorted.

Big mistake, he realized when her eyes narrowed again. She didn't say anything, just glared at him as she took another slow sip.

"I like your dog," Ozzie blurted out.

Stupid. Stupid. Stu— His trail of thought shattered as he watched her face light up. Until that moment, he had been half-convinced she wasn't capable of making a real smile.

"His name is Buck. And he's the best boy who ever existed. Ever. I will fight you on that."

A smile and a joke? Ozzie almost puffed out his chest with pride. *Now we're getting somewhere.*

"Well, obviously he is," Ozzie chuckled.

"Does he bite?" Ethan asked, trying to keep the light tone.

"Well, obviously he does," Basheba said. "But only when I tell him to."

Okay, two jokes. One's a little dark, but that's still a good sign. His hopes were confirmed when her smile grew, and she tilted her head to the side, her tangled gold hair spilling over one narrow shoulder.

"He's a guard dog. Very well trained."

"I see," Ha-Yun said. "He looks like a lovely animal."

She beamed, one hand lovingly rubbing the dog's neck. "Yes, he is. And beautifully brutal."

Percival took half a step closer to her and lowered his voice, almost as if he was trying to keep everyone else from hearing them.

"I didn't get a chance to say it last year. I'm very sorry for your loss."

Almost instantly, her pale eyes brightened with threatening tears. She bit her lips and nodded rapidly.

"Johnny was a good man. He was the best of us."

"Yes." Life came back to Basheba. Her cheeks warmed, and she concealed every trace of emotion behind a tiny, ever-present smile. "He was."

Ozzie had the distinct impression he was missing some integral piece of information; something important that would explain the way she locked her gaze onto Percival as she took another mouthful. He had never seen the man look so unsure. He shuffled his feet but was kept from having to come up with a response when she abruptly scanned the crowd.

"So, you finally got to bring Osgood–"

"Ozzie." He regretted correcting his name when Basheba turned her attention back to him.

One blink and she went from staring him down to looking like the most approachable person he had ever met. *Is it possible to get emotional whiplash?*

"Ozzie. Right, sorry, I'll get it. Don't you worry. So, what finally brings you onto our little farm of crazy?"

Ozzie cleared his throat. *Is there a way you're supposed to say it?* Not thinking of one, he settled for holding up the music box.

"Ah. I was hoping you were holding that for a friend."

"Nope. Just me."

"How old are you?"

"Almost sixteen."

Her eyelids fluttered closed, effectively keeping any other trace of emotion contained. There was just that smile. *The creepy, creepy doll smile.*

"Well." Her eyes opened, and she said it so delightfully, Ozzie could almost hear bells chiming in her words. "You're going to die. Enjoy your last day on earth. Well, last without all the nightmare-inducing stuff."

With a salute of her bottle, she was gone, disappearing into the crowd as a stranger appeared behind Ozzie.

"Don't worry about my niece," the man replied. He was pretty much just a scrawny frame topped with wire rim glasses and wrapped in a tweed coat. "Go on, get some sleep. The others won't be here for a while yet."

The reassurance flooded Ozzie's insides with warmth. As small as it was, it was the first hint from someone outside his family that everything was going to be okay. He desperately wanted to believe it. But there was something in the way Percival lifted his chin that made him hesitate. The tiny motion spoke volumes to Ozzie. *He doesn't trust this man. There's real hatred there.*

"Oh, thank you," Ha-Yun stammered.

Ethan rushed forward to grab the man's hand, shaking it almost violently in his gratitude. Only afterward did he recall that they were lacking some introductions.

"I'm sorry. I'm Ethan, this is my wife, Ha-Yun, and our son, Ozzie."

Ozzie's stomach tied up in knots as he watched his parents stammer and gush their gratitude on the stranger. He had never seen them this desperate. The truth sliced into him like a knife. *They're terrified. They don't think I'm going to survive. They think I'm going to die here.* Suddenly, the air seemed too thin to breathe.

"Oh, Percival has kept us well apprised of all of you," the man smiled. "I'm Isaac Bell. Have you met my daughter yet? A sweet girl called Claudia?"

"No, we've just arrived," Ha-Yun said.

Isaac's smile grew warmer while the tendons in Percival's neck pressed against his skin.

"You must be exhausted. I know my home won't be up to your normal standards, but it's close, warm, and yours to use as you wish."

"That's very kind," Ethan said. "Thank you. But I don't think any of us can sleep right now."

"You'll be surprised. Come, I'll introduce you to my daughter, and we'll get you comfortable. I'm sure Percival has a lot he needs to get in order."

"Thank you. But we really should be talking to Basheba," Ha-Yun said.

Isaac dismissed the protest with a wave. "She'll protect your son. I'll make sure of it."

It hadn't occurred to Ozzie how desperate his parents were for any kind of reassurance until he watched them both gush gratitude onto the stranger without any further prompting. Ozzie lingered back as Isaac herded his parents across the open field, waiting for them to be far enough away so they wouldn't hear his whisper to Percival.

"Why don't you like this guy?"

"Because he's a horrible human being," Percival whispered back. "He has absolutely no control over his niece, by the way. I don't know what he's angling for, but there's no way he can deliver on what he's promising."

"So, I should still be trying to win over Basheba?"

Percival mulled the question over before giving a quick shake of his head. "No. We can't, now. Any attempt to play nice will be tainted by Isaac."

Ozzie's stomach dropped. "What do we do then?"

"We need Cadwyn."

Chapter 9

Sheets of iron had replaced Cadwyn's eyelids. Muscle memory had long since taken over, keeping him upright on his bike even as he played with the brink of sleep. Reckless speeding hadn't been one of his best ideas, but it had shaved a few hours off his journey. The noonday sun had started to push into the afternoon by the time he reached the outskirts of the town.

The long, monotonous roads didn't help to keep his attention, but it did make it easier to ride. Looming trees shaded him from what little warmth the sun held. Combined with the air whipping around him, he was pretty sure he had fallen into a mild state of hypothermia. Although, that could've admittedly been a trick of his sleep-addled mind. While the demon had abandoned its trick of raining bloodied teeth upon him, the damage was done. His leather gloves crackled as he tightened his grip. It wasn't enough to stop his fingers from shaking.

Reducing his speed, he weaved through the cavernous jaws of the covered bridge. Chipped wooden planks, weather-worn and eaten away by burrowing insects, rattled under his wheels. The sound became a steady rhythm that mingled with the hum of his bike as he crossed over the babbling brook. Sunlight poured in between the old slabs of lumber that constructed the walls, cutting across the bridge in solid bars and flashing against his helmet's visor. The strobe light effect rendered him blind, leaving him to navigate by feel alone.

His bike growled in protest at the slower pace, but he didn't speed up. The ancient bridge was only large enough to accommodate one car at a time. If he was going to careen headfirst into a farmer's truck, it wasn't going to be at full speed. The sound of vibrating wood gave way to the crunch of dead leaves and the even feel of concrete. A twist of the wrist let him burst back out into the light. A small incline later, he was finally able to leave the river behind. *In the home stretch now.* The looming promise of sleep kept him moving. A few rapid blinks brought his eyes back into focus.

His brow knotted as he approached the first curve that marked the twisting road to come. A Witch Elm tree stood proudly in the arch of the bend. Its cluster base had been a formidable match for an old Chevrolet hatchback. The whole front of the car had crumbled like paper against the thick trunk, leaving glass scattered over the damp road and the weak headlights fighting against the shade cluster under the canopy.

Cadwyn slowed again, staring at the sight, trying to get his sluggish brain to make sense of it all, or at the very least, tell him why the sight left dread gnawing in the pit of his stomach.

1979 Chevrolet Chevette Hatchback. The information drifted across his mind before the meaning followed. *That's Basheba's car.*

Cadwyn gripped the brakes. The soft layer of leaves caught his wheels, making him skid and slide as he brought himself to a sudden halt.

Look around you! The thought tore free of the foggy haze that filled his skull. Still straddling his Thruxton, he tore his eyes off the mangled steel to survey his surroundings.

The forest stood tall and still around him. No witch. No demonic force. No Basheba. The kickstand struggled to keep the still rumbling vehicle upright as he leaped off and raced to the driver's side door.

No body. No blood.

The disjointed thoughts left Cadwyn sagging against the gaping hole of the window, trusting his thick leather jacket to protect him from the shards of glass that protruded from the frame like broken teeth.

She's not hurt.

He stared at the front seat, trying to understand why he cared about the scattered shrapnel. *It's undisturbed,* he realized at last. There was no sign anyone had been in the driver's seat at the time of impact. Gripping the door with both gloved hands, he cast a look down the road. It twisted out of sight after only a few yards.

Well, go, a voice in his head whispered, almost as if his inner self couldn't stand his sleepy stupidity for a moment longer. *If you hurry, you might be able to catch up with her.*

Before he could turn away, a clear bag of yogurt pretzels caught his eye. The combination of a long torso and a long reach made it easy for him to snatch up the bag from the back seat. *What on earth?* Vibrant green icing filled two of the pretzel holes, each glop topped with candy eyes to make them look like little aliens. A little ribbon kept the bag together and he twisted the attached tag around to read it.

"Intergalactic Truck Stop. Best stop on the Milky Way Highway," he read aloud. A soft chuckle rolled around the inside of his helmet. "Basheba, the places you go."

Struck with the sudden urge to try one, he pulled back away from the car. It wasn't until he was plucking at the drawstring that his situation dawned on him. This had all the makings of a trap.

Shoving the bag into one of his jacket pockets, he scanned the area with more concern. The tint of his visor muted the vibrant woods around him. It saved his eyes from the glare, but swelled the shadows, letting them gather beyond the initial tree line. The normal sounds of wildlife that would fill the woods were lost under the constant rumble of his bike. Robbed of both sight and sound, he retreated back to the road, constantly watching for any signs of movement.

Adrenaline ripped through his veins like wildfire, burning away any trace of fatigue and leaving his hands twitching. A few quick strides and he was back on his bike, gunning the engine until it howled like a wounded beast.

Nothing rushed from the undergrowth to prevent his escape. He didn't know if he should find that a comfort or a dark omen, but it didn't matter. All he wanted was to get to town.

Picking up his speed turned the slow, meandering curves of the road into dangerous turns. The road slashed at his knees as he leaned into them, stripping away the leather of his biker pants to grind against the internal padding. Bit by bit, it came closer to reaching his flesh.

A straight stretch allowed him to push his engine to its limits. Frozen air lashed at him. Shadows danced across his eyes, some coming from outside his visor while others seemed to be within his helmet. Decomposing leaves and mud spewed up from his wheels as he barreled down the foliage-covered road. The earth trembled, the trees thrashed violently, and, with an explosion of shattered twigs, a massive beast lumbered free of the tree line. Two swift strides brought the creature to the center of the road. Cadwyn jerked, forcing his bike into a skid and almost losing control entirely as he slid a few yards to an abrupt stop.

A fair distance still separated him from the beast, allowing him to see the colossal creature in its entirety. It had the body of a man, if the man was a gigantic bodybuilder. Swollen muscles twitched beneath skin stained with blood, mud, and sweat. Its shoulders were broad enough that its bull head wasn't out of proportion. Unknown muck matted the short fur that covered the minotaur's head and neck. Black eyes bulged from the brown fur, undeniably bovine, but still somehow conveying dark malice. Trails of steam worked its way from flaring nostrils, coiling in the chilled air before dissipating around its curved horns.

The minotaur hunched forward, dislodging the clumps of flesh previous kills had left clinging to the deadly peaks, allowing the putrid chunks to fall onto the earth between its feet. Cadwyn's heart hammered painfully against his ribs as the minotaur carefully lined its horns up for attack. Its bare, mud-encrusted feet scraped over the ground.

Cadwyn jerked hard on his heavy bike, balanced himself on the foot bars, and forced the acceleration to its breaking point. The back tire spun wild, forcing the whole bike to fishtail before it found traction and suddenly shot forward. He desperately searched for a way around the minotaur but found nothing. A part of him wanted to turn back, to take one of the other roads into town. But there was something heavy in the back of his mind that whispered he wouldn't make it across the stream again. Katrina wouldn't let him slip her trap so easily.

Demons can't touch you. His own thoughts sounded like they came from the far end of a tunnel. *Not until the box is open. The Witch is just trying to waste my time. Get to town.*

Heat pulsated from the motor as the bike snarled. The minotaur snorted, gushing clouds of steam into the air.

It can't touch you.

The bull charged forward to meet him. Its wild baying cut over the sound of the machinery. Impossibly large muscles bulged as it braced for impact. At the last moment, the minotaur swept its head out, ducked lower, and drove one huge horn into the Thruxton's front wheel. There wasn't time to feel the sudden jolt before he was airborne.

Crushing steel and the dying gasps of the bike clashed somewhere in the back of his awareness before he hit the ground. His helmet absorbed the worst of it and allowed his muscle memory to take over. Tucking in his limbs, he allowed himself to roll.

Leather ripped. His helmet snapped against the road until his visor was little more than a few shards of Perspex plastic left scattered along the path he had taken. At least, the momentum had drained away. Cadwyn rocked onto his shoulder but there wasn't enough energy behind him to complete the rotation. He flopped onto his back. A solid thud that pushed the last of the air from his lungs. It was a small relief to let his arms drop from his chest.

Nothing's broken.

He would have laughed if he had had breath to do so.

Writhing in pain, he felt his brain slosh around the inside of his skull. Pushing himself up onto his elbows, sucking in a deep breath, he glanced back down the road.

The minotaur thrashed wildly, working the remains of the bike off its horns. Frozen in horror, Cadwyn watched, witnessing the creature's strength as it hurled the mangled bike into the woods without ever placing a hand upon it.

With a thunderous bellow, it turned back to Cadwyn and charged. Cadwyn forced himself up. Every joint in his body screamed in pain. Blood oozed through the places the leathers hadn't been able to properly protect. Cadwyn ripped off his helmet, keeping it gripped tightly in his arms as he sprinted to meet the creature.

At the last moment, the bull once again lowered its head. Cadwyn dropped lower. Due to the beast's colossal size, he was able to pass between its legs. With every ounce of force he had within his power, Cadwyn drove his helmet into the minotaur's crotch.

A pained sound cracked through the silence. Its legs wobbled, its balance thrown off by the abrupt strike and resounding pain. While it toppled forward, Cadwyn got back up onto his feet and spun. The beast was already reaching for him, forcing him to retreat instead of striking its throat as he had intended.

Avoiding one arm brought him into contact with a horn. The razor-sharp tip easily severed his protective leathers and slashed across his chest. Cadwyn ignored the pain and latched onto the horn, forcing the entire weight of his body against it, trying to push the bull's head down. The minotaur merely stretched its neck. But he had his opportunity again.

Grasping the horn with both hands, he drove his knee up. What remained of the protective padding added to the blow and muffled the feel of the beast's crunching larynx. Steam spilled from its mouth to fill the air. It thrashed wildly, easily tossing Cadwyn aside as it choked.

Get up. Get up.

Cadwyn took the blow and scrambled to his feet, desperate not to miss the opening, knowing he might not get another chance. He swung the helmet with both hands. This time, it cracked against the minotaur's eye. The resulting spike of pain and disorientation bought him another few seconds.

Don't let him get off his knees.

Cadwyn shrank back to avoid the wild limbs before surging

forward. The combination of his body weight and the creature's confusion helped him bring it down. It took every muscle Cadwyn had, straining to the point of breaking, to crack the minotaur's skull against the road. But the first victory gave him an opening for the next.

Fall back. Strike again.

It was a method that had been trained into him to bring down the people he worked with, but never with this violence. The first streams of blood made Cadwyn gag. His natural instincts told him to stop each time the wounded beast released an animalistic cry.

Fall back. Strike again!

The solid crack of bone became a wet crunch. Blood, brains, and hunks of furry flesh clung to his skin. Pain and fatigue made his arms wobble, forcing him to release the horns in favor of the helmet. Cadwyn hit the beast's skull until it lost all shape, and then continued until his helmet cracked and splintered into useless shards. He hit until he was physically incapable of lifting his arms again.

The minotaur had long since stopped moving by the time Cadwyn flopped back. Thin wisps of steam snaked up from the fresh blood that pooled around him. It was impossible to tell which one of them it belonged to. Adrenaline faded, pain returned, and he found himself barely able to link together a single thought. All he could do was breathe.

His unfocused gaze stared at the canopy above them; blood red leaves shivering against a covering of dense grey clouds. At first, he didn't notice it. Then he absently assumed it was a misfiring of his obviously bruised brain. Red and blue light danced around him, flashed across the trees, and tainted his view.

It wasn't until he heard the crunch of footsteps that it occurred to him it could be on the outside of his malfunctioning brain. He blinked and the feet came to a stop by his skull. He had to squint in order to bring the police officer into view.

"What the hell happened here?" The officer asked.

Cadwyn's mouth jerked into a half smile. "Hi, Trevor. How're the kids?"

Chapter 10

Mina sat at the small table by the window. Sunlight streamed through the polished glass, giving her all she needed to study the box in detail. It was the first time she had been able to get a good look at it. Tradition dictated the cube was to be instantly sealed within a thick iron box, the kind used for radioactive material. She had always been told the Selected was allowed to take it back out once they were far enough away from the children. However, that didn't seem to be the case. Her father had refused to even let her near it until they were within the town's café, curiously named Witch's Brew. He had disappeared out the back with her other relatives shortly after they had arrived, leaving Jeremiah with strict instructions to keep her from opening the container. That had lasted only as long as it took for her to reach across the booth.

After studying each side in turn, she had come to one conclusion; she should have bought that magnifying glass keychain she had seen in the store before. Suddenly, it seemed completely practical, and not dorky at all. Growling in frustration, Mina sat back and thought, then shot a question at her brother.

"Do you have your phone on you?"

Jeremiah jolted at the sudden address. "Don't you?"

"It's charging in my bedroom."

Cautiously, her big brother slipped off the distant table and inched his way across the room.

"Don't you dare take the box," she warned him.

"I don't want to touch that thing."

He fished his phone from his back pocket and held it out with the tips of his fingers, keeping himself as far away from the table as he could without throwing his birthday present. Mina struggled to keep from rolling her eyes.

"Can you open it for me, please?"

After unlocking it, he presented it in exactly the same way as before.

"Thanks." She pulled the phone away and quickly clicked off a few photographs.

"What are you doing?" Jeremiah asked.

"I need a magnifying glass."

"You're taking photos," he said.

The stress must be getting to him.

"So I can magnify them," she replied.

He still wasn't getting it. The box held the full focus of his attention, his eyes wide and his breathing shallow.

"You know, zoom in."

"Oh, right," he mumbled absently.

Mina picked up the box to shift the angle of her photographs.

"Do you have to keep touching that thing?" He still had enough sense to keep his voice down.

Neither of them wanted to know just how mad their dad would be to learn that the box was outside the container.

"I want to get a better look at this pattern. It keeps moving."

"What pattern?"

"These squiggles." She zoomed in on one of her photographs to show him what she meant. "See, here? Under the shifting metal bars."

Jeremiah craned his neck to see the screen but didn't dare come any closer to the box.

"Oh, yeah," he murmured.

"At first, I thought they were just decoration. But there's no repetition. The same symbols, odd spacing, not repeating," she thought aloud.

"What are you babbling about?"

She finally looked up. "I think it's a language."

"A language?"

"A language hidden under moving elements on a box with no seams." She couldn't help but feel a bit impressed. "Who would go to this much effort for a prop?"

Jeremiah glared at her. "Are you kidding me? You still think this is fake?"

"Not fake exactly," she admitted. "But exaggerated."

"You were locked in a closet with her."

Mina threw herself back in her seat, remembering just in time not to toss his phone across the room, even if it would have been dramatically fitting.

"I have claustrophobia. You know that. Being in that closet..." She shuddered under the memories that began to prick at the corners of her mind but forced herself to continue. *You need to appear strong if he's going to take you seriously.* "In those circumstances, it would be completely normal for someone with my condition to exaggerate certain things, or even outright hallucinate."

Jeremiah slumped down on a nearby chair. Then, deeming that wasn't enough, smacked his head down against the matching tabletop.

"Everything I experienced can be explained," she insisted.

"What about the box?!" he bellowed to the ceiling, raising his hands for good measure.

She scoffed. "Obviously, it was in the closest before I got there."

Jeremiah released a sound akin to a dying animal as he began to smack his head upon the table repeatedly. Before he could gather himself enough to actually speak, the door to the kitchen swung open and a short girl rushed in.

Mina eyed the Rottweiler that trotted at the girl's side rather than the girl herself. There was something about the gigantic canine that put her on edge. The door smacked open again, letting a boy follow her.

"Basheba! Hey, wait up," the young Korean man called.

The girl in question slowed her pace but didn't stop. "Can you be quick? I've got to go run an errand."

"Well, can I come with you?" His initial nervousness evaporated behind a brilliant smile. "I just thought it would be cool if we could hang out for a bit. You know, get to know each other."

"Why would I want to do that?"

The question left the boy stuck in a state of stunned sputtering. Basheba didn't wait around for him to gather his senses. She was opening the door when she noticed Mina and Jeremiah on the far side of the room.

"Oh, hey!" The boy beamed. "You're Mina, right? I'm Ozzie. We're going into the woods together. Part of the creepy box club. I can mention that in front of him, right?"

"You really can't handle awkward silences, can you?" Basheba asked, watching him from the corner of her eyes.

Mina decided it was best to ignore the snide comment. "This is my brother, Jeremiah. And, yes, he knows all about it."

"What are you doing with your music box?" Ozzie asked, clearly desperate to keep the conversation going.

"Examining it. Would you like to join us?"

"Sure," he said before casting a quick glance to Basheba, almost like asking permission.

"You go right ahead," she said, pulling the door open wider.

"Who's going with you?" Jeremiah asked quickly.

She tilted her head to indicate the dog.

Jeremiah looked to all of them in turn before stammering. "You're one of the Selected. You can't be alone."

"Buck's way more loyal than anyone else around here," she dismissed. "But if it makes you feel better, I'm on my way to pick up Cadwyn."

Ozzie perked up at the name. "Cad?"

"Yeah."

"Picking him up from where?" Mina asked.

"Local jail." She wiggled her mobile phone in the air. "Apparently, they're refusing to let him go without proper supervision."

"You count as proper supervision?" Ozzie asked while Mina inquired about the charges.

Basheba rolled her eyes.

"I'll come with you," Ozzie said.

It took Mina a second to make a decision. Each one of them had a box, so she wouldn't lose the opportunity to study it. On the other hand, being able to question the other Selected like this was likely to pass her by if she stayed. Soon enough, they'd be hiking through the backwoods. *Not an ideal environment to get the truth from anyone*, she determined. Additionally, her parents wouldn't be around to interfere.

"I'd like to stretch my legs."

"Mina," Jeremiah whispered sharply.

"Aren't I supposed to work with them? Isn't that an integral part of this?" she argued.

"But–"

"I'll be okay."

"You say that."

She held up one hand in the Scout's honor salute. "I promise I'll stay with the group at all times."

Jeremiah chewed on his inner cheeks. "Okay. There and back. Give me my phone and if anything happens, have Basheba call me. Got it?"

"Got it." Mina stood up and took a few steps toward the door, before it occurred to her. "Don't tell dad."

"I might not be book smart like you, but I'm not a complete idiot."

To offer him a small measure of reassurance, she closed the radioactive metal box and took the music one with her. Absently rolling the phone over and over between his hands, he offered her a weak smile and watched her go. They had barely gotten a yard away from the café door before Jeremiah raced after them.

"What's wrong?"

Jeremiah drew her into a crushing hug, his arms shaking as badly as his stammered breaths.

"Just come back, Mina. Okay? Come back."

"I will. I promise." *None of this is real,* she told herself sharply. And she meant it. Every word. But that didn't stop her from returning his hug with matching intensity. "Just keep dad out of my hair for a bit, okay?"

"Yeah. And I'll keep the tide from going out, too," Jeremiah snorted.

Finally, he let go and rushed back into the café. A cold chill swept down her spine when he was out of sight. *It's nothing. You're just being paranoid.* Righting her thoughts, she crammed the box into her jacket pocket, forcing the seams to their snapping point. Ozzie gave her a warm smile when she finally looked away from the Witch's Brew.

"So." She tried to sound as casual as possible. "Where's the police station?"

Ozzie's thick dark eyebrows knitted together.

"I only found out this place existed yesterday," he chuckled nervously. "I thought you'd know the way. I mean, I know you haven't gone into the woods before, but you come here every year, don't you?"

"No. This is my first time in Black River."

"Oh."

For a split second, the warmth in Ozzie's dark eyes flickered like a small flame in the wind. It allowed her to see the fear he had kept hidden beneath. A sharp breath and the warm was back.

"Neither of us should be in charge of the map, huh?"

Rattled by what she had seen, Mina struggled to return his smile. "I guess so."

"Hey, Basheba?"

They both turned to discover the short girl was already halfway down Main Street. They had to run to catch up. Mina had to hand it to Basheba. It took a certain level of commitment to remain completely oblivious to two people standing only a few feet away. Ozzie's first few attempts to draw her into conversation fell flat and he was soon grappling for topics.

"Looks like she's been here a bit," Ozzie said to Mina. "We should definitely give her the compass."

Basheba turned down a side street, absentmindedly giving her dog a playful nudge and smiling at his overreaction.

Mina took pity on him and decided to take a run at Basheba herself. "I was told you've been in the woods before."

The dog paid more attention to them than its owner did.

"Have I done something to upset you?" Ozzie asked.

"No," Basheba replied.

While she didn't turn around, she did manage to sound honestly confused as to how he could have come to such a conclusion. Mina and Ozzie shared a glance, each clearly hoping the other would somehow know how to handle the small woman.

Before they could sort out a plan of attack, they had reached the police station. A reception desk separated the small waiting area from the larger back. A few scattered desks filled the space, topped with more books and takeaway containers than paperwork. A row of thick black bars turned the back corner into a series of holding cells.

"You can't just walk back there," Mina whispered harshly.

It wasn't a surprise that Basheba didn't listen. She pushed through the low swinging gate and into the back office. Her dog leaped the aged wood to follow.

"Ladies first?" Ozzie said with a shrug.

It was getting harder for Mina to keep a tight grip on the frustration growing inside of her. "This is how people get shot."

"Huh. Hey, what do you think will happen if we were shot before we have to go into the woods?"

Mina fled from that question by grudgingly trailing along behind the older girl, leaving Ozzie to follow. Almost in unison, they entered the restricted area and the staff bathroom door flung open. Ozzie jerked back a step, as if contemplating outrunning the law enforcement officer. Holding up one hand to steady him, Mina straightened her spine and fixed a gentle but polite smile upon her lips. Before she could speak, however, Basheba greeted the man with an energetic and almost childish glee.

"Trevor! I missed you!"

She raced to the man. Instead of surprise, the taller man scooped down and caught her around the hip, lifting her clean off her feet. One quick spin, and he placed her back down.

"Oh, look at you. You must have grown half a foot," Trevor beamed, ruffling her hair. His skin seemed a dozen shades darker against her golden hair.

"Does he know she's in her twenties?" Ozzie whispered in Mina's ear.

Mina shook her head, captivated by the sight before her, "I don't think he does."

"Now, what are you doing here?"

Basheba giggled and clasped her hands behind her back, twisting her torso like a proud child.

"I'm here to pick up Cadwyn."

Trevor frowned, "He called you?"

"Why wouldn't he?" Basheba pouted.

Suspicion crossed his face, and she matched it. However, she kept a certain adorable charm to her glare, which soon had the man chuckling.

"I'm sure you know what you're doing, little poppet," Trevor dismissed.

Crouching down, he called the dog over. The move effectively hid his face from Mina's line of sight and kept her from getting a good read on the man. The towering beast of a dog wallowed happily in the officer's attention, tongue lolling out the side of its jaws and tail whipping about as he leaned into the body rubs.

"Who's this gorgeous boy?"

"That's my dog, Buck," Basheba beamed with pride.

Mina managed to catch Basheba's gaze over the distracted officer's shoulders. The innocent façade slipped like a mask to reveal a small smirk. No more than that. But it spoke volumes and made a slither of ice coil in the pit of her stomach. The front door burst open, allowing a very loud elderly woman to come waddling inside. Trevor's head snapped up and Basheba instantly resumed her performance.

"I've got to go take care of that."

"Okie dokie," Basheba chirped.

The officer barely hesitated before holding up his hand, the cell key dangling from one finger.

"You need to give this back to me before you go."

Basheba nodded rapidly, sending her hair flying. "I will. Cross my heart and hope to die."

"Good girl." He placed the key in Basheba's cupped hands and headed off to the front of the station.

The second his back was turned, Basheba's smile dropped, her eyes grew cold, and she stalked toward the cells.

Mina rushed to catch up. "Exactly how old does he think you are?"

"No idea," she dismissed. "If I ask, people start looking at the details and it spoils the illusion."

Ozzie joined the group. "I always hate it when people think I'm a kid."

"You are a kid," Basheba said.

"And why tell the truth when the lie lets you manipulate a police officer?" Mina added.

For once, the blonde paused and turned toward her. "You disapprove?"

"I do."

Basheba hummed thoughtfully. "It's a good thing I don't care about your opinion then, isn't it? Otherwise, you might have actually hurt my feelings."

"What is it people say about burning bridges?" The voice drifted groggily to them from the furthest cell. The one tucked into the corner.

"That it makes good kindling?" Basheba replied.

The roll of her eyes wasn't enough to hide her smile. It was small but honest and instantly spiked Mina's curiosity. She decided to keep her mouth shut and watch the interaction unfold.

A mound that Mina had mistaken as blankets heaved as a man worked his way out from under it. Rich brown hair flopped over his forehead in sweaty strips. A fledgling bruise had started to claim the sharp peak of his right cheekbone. The remains of a nosebleed stained his upper lip and dried blood coated his shirt. Finally succeeding in freeing his long legs, he hunched forward and braced his elbows on his knees.

"What happened to you?" Ozzie asked.

"I beat a minotaur to death with my helmet," Cadwyn grinned. "How was your morning?"

"A real minotaur?" Mina snapped despite herself.

"You killed it?" Ozzie asked.

Basheba straightened, "Are those my pretzels?"

Chapter 11

"Wait, you weren't arrested?" Ozzie asked, squinting as they left the station and reentered the sunlight. He kept glancing over his shoulder, sure Trevor would chase them down. "I thought you were arrested. Don't you have to sign something or talk to someone?"

Cadwyn smiled as he stretched his arms over his head. His teeth were long, sharper than the norm, and slightly stained pink with blood. Ozzie averted his gaze to the Halloween decorated streets, trying to quell the queasy feeling steadily trickling into his stomach.

"Trevor wouldn't dare cross me after what happened last time," Basheba commented.

Ozzie's gut tightened. "What happened last time?"

Cadwyn stifled his humor to give him an actual answer. "She's just messing with you, Ozzie. Which is mean."

He clearly said the last sentence in reprimand of Basheba. She ignored him.

"I wasn't arrested," Cadwyn continued. "Trevor was just letting me sleep in the cells until he could hand off responsibility of me to someone else."

"Responsibility?" Mina pushed.

"Black River doesn't have a hospital, and the local doctor is a quack. I refused to see him."

"I don't get it," Ozzie said.

"Having found him, Trevor would have a duty of care over Cadwyn," Mina explained. "Cadwyn has a right to refuse medical treatment, of course. But can you imagine the legal and ethical nightmare Trevor would find himself in if he just let Cadwyn wander around and die of his injuries?"

Ozzie gave that some thought. "So, Trevor's covering his butt? Why couldn't you just say that?"

Mina takes herself too seriously. The glare she threw Ozzie's way made that little bit of information blatantly clear. Shrinking away from her annoyance, Ozzie found his attention drawn to Cadwyn's blood-soaked shirt.

The man's biker gear had protected most of his body, but it gaped in the front where it had been slashed open, allowing glimpses of the bandages wrapped around his torso. The majority of the material was still pristine, white as snow against the midnight black of his leathers. But blood had started to seep through to the surface. Little crimson dots that seemed to grow before Ozzie's eyes. The vibrant color filled his vision.

"Maybe we should take you to the doctor," Ozzie said before swallowing thickly.

Cadwyn made a sneak attack for Basheba's yogurt pretzels. It earned him an elbow to the ribs. Not hard, just enough to make him jerk away. The motion must have reopened the wound because fresh blood pushed against his bandages.

"You're bleeding," Ozzie said weakly.

"It's just a little seepage. Completely normal for new stitches," Cadwyn assured.

The comment drew Mina's attention. "Trevor knows that kind of first aid?"

"No," he chuckled. "I did it myself."

After being rebuffed from the snacks, Cadwyn began rummaging through the bright red bag he had retrieved from Trevor's desk before they left. Ozzie had dismissed the fat backpack as Cadwyn's luggage, but now, as the older man searched through the numerous pockets, he caught sight of the medical symbol embroidered on the top. *A medical bag,* he realized. Ozzie found himself strangely disappointed. *It doesn't look like the ones they use in the movies.* With a grunt of victory, the nurse pulled free what he had been searching for. A beaten-up pack of cigarettes.

"Maybe we should still take you to a doctor," Ozzie said.

"Why does no one take my degree seriously?" he mumbled around a cigarette, already fumbling with a lighter.

"They do," Basheba said. "They just don't take *you* seriously."

One well-practiced strike of his thumb got his Zippo to work, and he glared at her over the steady flame.

"Thanks for the clarification."

"Anytime." Basheba's smile faded when the tall man managed to snatch a handful of the pretzels out of the bag.

"I will burn you," Basheba declared. "Don't try me."

The threat made Ozzie's chest tighten. He didn't doubt for a moment that she meant it. Cadwyn, however, only chuckled. Even though he towered over the woman beside him, the nurse still tilted his head back to blow a lungful of smoke into the air.

Mina cocked her head to the side, "You're a medical professional."

"So I know exactly how bad this is." With the slender cigarette nipped between two fingers, he took a long drag and blew the smoke above them once more. "Don't smoke kids."

While his words remained playful, there was an undeniable shift in Cadwyn's tone. Something colder. Almost bitter. *Don't judge their coping mechanisms.*

"I need either a nap or a coffee," Cadwyn said, gingerly rolling his shoulders. He exchanged his cigarette with a pretzel. "These things don't have enough sugar to keep me awake."

"If we survive, you're buying me a new pack," Basheba grumbled.

"A minotaur ran you off the road!" Mina's enraged outburst made everyone flinch.

Their small group stopped in the middle of a residential street and turned their attention to her.

"That's right," Cadwyn said.

Mina's jaw dropped. "You expect us to believe that?"

"Why would I lie?"

Don't bring me into this, Ozzie silently pleaded. It didn't stop Mina from turning to him for backup.

"Can't you see none of this makes sense?"

Ozzie winced, not sure what to say, or whom he was better off isolating.

"Where do I even start?" she declared.

Cadwyn took another deep draw of his cigarette and said, "Throw them at me in any order."

"All right." Planting her feet, she crossed her arms over her chest. "How did you survive a bike crash with only minor injuries?"

If Mina was expecting a reaction beyond a smirk, she was disappointed.

"Everyone in the four families should know how to fall. Not that the additional training didn't help."

"Someone trained you?" Mina asked. "To fall?"

"Fall, absorb impact, take the pain and keep going," he nodded.

"That's some strange training for a nurse, isn't it?"

Basheba didn't stop chewing as she cut in, "He's a psych nurse at a hospital for the criminally insane. Don't you know violence against medical professionals is a real problem?"

"Besides that, bikes are death traps. No one should ride one unless they know how to crash them." Almost as if he had momentarily forgotten about Mina, he turned to the short girl beside him. "Now that your car's totaled, are you going to get a bike? Maybe a side cart for Buck? Ginger's expanding *Ride or Die*. She'll have room for you in the program."

"I sleep in my car."

"It sounds so sad when you say it like that."

"You should give Ginger a call. She might make you her poster boy." Basheba raised her hands for emphasis. "My program kept this idiot alive."

"Slightly hurtful."

Mina's frustrated groan brought the pair back into her interrogation.

"For the sake of argument, I'll concede you know how to fall and that was enough to save you. It's a long shot, but okay."

"That's clearly the sound of conceding," Basheba noted.

"How did you kill it with your bare hands?"

"Determination and a deep reservoir of resentment," Cadwyn mumbled around his quickly disappearing cigarette.

"From what I remember, minotaurs are heavily muscled beasts," Mina pressed. "It's a little unbelievable someone like you could kill one with your bare hands, don't you think?"

As subtly as he could, Ozzie inched a bit further away from Mina's side, not wanting to get caught up in the dark looks that were now being sent in her direction. Especially since Basheba started that creepy smiling again.

"And what do you think I can kill?" Basheba asked.

Mina ignored the question and switched tactics. "And your whole story goes against the established legends. I've always been told the demons can't cause physical injury until the box is opened."

Basheba laughed. A sweet little cackle that held an edge of mania. It was Cadwyn who replied.

"We're in Black River, Mina. I was passing by the Witch Woods."

"So?"

Instantly, Basheba's humor fell away. "You have to be kidding me. Didn't your daddy teach you anything?"

"The Witch Woods is Katrina's home turf. She can do things there that she can't do anywhere else."

"With all due respect, Cadwyn, what does that mean?"

"It means if you can't wrap your brilliant mind around the idea of a guy with a bull head, you're not going to last," Basheba said, her humor flooding back into her voice.

Mina bristled, the muscles in her jaw twitched as she met Basheba's cool gaze.

"Cadwyn," Mina said, still staring at the small girl before her. "You killed it. Then Trevor found you. Is that right?"

"Yes."

"Then Trevor must have seen the corpse. He didn't strike me as a man who has just seen a mythical beast brought to life."

It clearly enraged Mina that Basheba lazily selected another pretzel. She shifted her weight from one foot to the other, her pretty face growing taut.

If Basheba noticed, she didn't care. "It's almost as if it's not the weirdest thing he's seen around these parts."

"Then where is it?" Mina snapped. "There has to be a corpse. He wouldn't have just left it on the road for anyone to find. So where's the body, Basheba?"

"Because that's something she would know," Cadwyn cut in.

Basheba grunted, took her time swallowing, then said, "Funeral home."

Doubt crossed Mina's face for the first time. "I'm not sure I follow."

"Well, let's use logic," Basheba said, paying more attention to her dwindling rations. "There's no hospital around these parts. The funeral home is the only place decked out to take care of a corpse if they felt like holding onto it. If they don't, the crematorium and graveyard are nice and close."

Nonchalantly, she stared at the woman and continued munching.

"I'm just guessing this last bit, but I'm envisioning this thing as being really buff. Heavy. Not something you can shove into the back of a police cruiser. So that big old hearse the funeral home has would be pretty convenient for transportation." She turned abruptly to Cadwyn. "These things are making me thirsty, have you got any water?"

He quickly produced a bottle and handed it over. "You know, that's a pretty good idea."

Somehow, she managed to hum quizzically while chugging half of the bottle's contents.

He lowered his voice to elaborate. "They do have a distinct lack of practical experience."

Once more, Ozzie found his thoughts spiraling beyond his control. All that toppled out of his mouth was, "I can see it?"

"Funeral home's right around the corner," Cadwyn said cheerfully.

Basheba released a disgruntled humph.

"What else have you got to do with your day?" Cadwyn asked.

"Sleep, mostly."

"Damn, that does sound good."

"No, this will be very educational," Mina cut in. She smiled up at the towering man. "Please, show me the minotaur."

It then turned into a staring contest between the two girls, each one daring the other to back down. Eventually, Basheba smiled. Small and sweet and with a predatory edge.

"You know what? Let's go. There is no foreseeable way this could go wrong."

Mina's unspoken confidence only grew when Basheba turned on one delicate heel and stalked off, Buck trotting along beside her.

Cadwyn cringed as he watched her go. "That right there is the air horn of warning signs. We probably should change our plans before we see what she's thinking."

"I'd like to see it," Mina declared.

Keeping her spine rod straight, she stomped off after Basheba. Ozzie wasn't sure what he was supposed to do, so he was grateful when Cadwyn patted him on the back of his shoulder. He offered him a warm smile.

"I guess we should catch up with them before they get themselves into trouble."

He couldn't argue with that. *We have to get them on the same page,* Ozzie thought desperately as he followed behind the girls. But no matter how hard he thought about it, he couldn't come up with a way to get them to that point.

Basheba cut across the road, rounded a corner, and followed the new street until the forest blocked their way. A quaint white house stood alone to their right. It was pressed slightly into the woods, making room for the graveyard that started before them and rolled up over a nearby hill. Gray stones dotted the frost-bitten grass. Most were chipped and dulled by centuries of storms and had sunken into the earth to stand at strange angles. A few still held their original polish. It was easy to pick them out when the sun peeked from behind the gathering clouds to make them glisten.

People milled around the gravestones, some following tour guides in brightly colored coats while others made their own way around. A few graves in particular seemed to draw their attention. They clustered around the stones, posing for photos before swarming in like bees. Ozzie was too busy trying to figure out what they were doing to notice that Basheba had stopped walking.

"Sorry," he mumbled after colliding into her back.

Basheba didn't acknowledge him. A deep flush steadily crept into her cheeks as she watched the flow of tourists. It looked like she was going to scream. The illusion ended when she choked down a staggered breath.

She's trying not to cry, Ozzie realized.

"What are they doing?" he asked aloud.

"A few of our relatives are buried up there," Cadwyn said.

Ozzie looked from the people to Basheba and back.

"I don't get it."

"We're a tourist attraction," Cadwyn answered in a whisper. "The cursed lines of the Bell Witch."

"Are they putting chalk on one?"

The older man held off answering until he had snubbed out his first cigarette and lit a new one.

"That's Katrina's grave," he said, once again blowing the fumes above their heads. "Recently put up, of course. Convicted witches weren't buried on hallowed ground."

"Are they leaving a mark?"

"Oh, that's new, too. Leave a mark and get a wish. I haven't got a clue who came up with that."

Suddenly, Basheba burst into motion. Only Buck had anticipated it and she was entering the graveyard gates before the others thought to follow. They somehow managed to lose her within the thin crowd.

"There!" Mina said.

She pointed up the hill. It was easier to notice Buck's black coat than the blonde.

"What's she holding?" Mina asked.

"A rake?" Ozzie suggested.

Cadwyn broke into a sprint. "She found the gardener's shed."

A tour had just started up the hill, the meandering guests blocking Ozzie and Mina's path and slowed them down enough that they only got halfway up before chaos broke out. Shouts of protests and demands for answers were covered by Buck's menacing snarls.

Mina abruptly grabbed Ozzie's wrist and brought him to a stop. Side by side, they watched as Basheba attacked a gravestone with the metal teeth of the rake, chipping off pieces with every swing. Cadwyn swooped in to block off the few people brave enough to risk Buck's wrath. Eventually, she drove the tip of the rake into the soft earth by the base of the headstone. It took all of her weight bearing down on the opposite end to leverage it out.

With a few startled cries, the stone toppled, flopping down the hillside with heavy thuds. Basheba wiped the sweat from her forehead, tossed the rake aside, and started back down to the main gate as if nothing had happened.

She walked over the fallen stone and made it back to Mina and Ozzie before the crowd caught up with her. Buck and Cadwyn still tried to hold them back, but it was an impossible task. Now that they were close enough, Ozzie could pick a few sentences out from the general, belligerent noise.

"What the hell is your problem?" A woman screamed, pushing aside Cadwyn's arm to get a few steps closer. "I'm calling the police."

"Fine," Basheba dismissed.

"Who do you think you are?"

Ozzie couldn't pinpoint who had spoken, but Basheba whirled on them like an angered snake, reared up and ready to strike.

"That bitch doesn't get to be buried near my family!" Each word cracked like thunder. Far louder than her small form would give credit for.

The stunned silence didn't last. Like coming rain, the questions were sporadic at first and then joined into a sudden downpour. Some wanted to know which of the four families she belonged to. Others asked for a photograph, while even more amongst them moved about the phones they were recording with to try and catch her face. Basheba shouldered past Ozzie and Mina.

"Let's go."

It was Buck more than Cadwyn who kept the crowd from following them from the graveyard. With fang and threat, he blocked the way until the group had reformed by the funeral home. The door wasn't locked. Basheba flung it open before whistling softly. Buck yelped in acknowledgment and raced toward them, paws kicking up clumps of earth and head lowered with dedicated purpose.

"Good job!" Basheba bent over and opened her arms wide, welcoming the slobbering, excitable dog into her embrace. Her voice was light but crackled around the edges. "Who's the best boy in the whole wide world?"

"Is it me?" Cadwyn asked as he closed the door behind them, fixing the lock just in case anyone thought to follow.

"You're lovely and all." She dropped into baby talk and cupped Buck's floppy cheeks. "But how can you compete with this face? Look at it. Look at his beautiful face."

"Well, you have me there."

She wrapped her arms around Buck's neck. The dog accepted the embrace, standing strong like a sentinel as Basheba progressively looked smaller. Ozzie shuffled his weight and locked his eyes onto the floor. The small sign of vulnerability was obviously not meant to be viewed by anyone, least of all a stranger like him. *I wonder if her dad's grave is up there.*

"That was a crime," Mina declared, breaking the uneasy silence. "You can't just destroy property like that."

Basheba rolled her eyes. "Who's going to stop me?"

Mina crossed her arms over her chest. "You might have to spend the night in jail."

"Good," she responded. In response to their startled looks, she said, "What? I don't want to stay with my uncle and the hotel doesn't take dogs. The cell is kind of my best option."

It was the first opening Ozzie had found to make himself useful, and he latched onto it. "I'll make sure the hotel takes you and Buck in. Don't worry about it."

"Exactly how can you do that?" Mina challenged.

Ozzie shrugged one shoulder. "If all else fails, I'll buy the place."

"I always forget how rich you guys are," Cadwyn noted. "If we're going to see the bull, we probably should get moving. One of those guys is definitely going to call the cops."

"We can't just walk down there," Mina said.

Basheba smirked and stalked across the room. "Again, I ask, who's going to stop me?"

"Whoever locked the door," Mina replied.

Both Basheba and Cadwyn broke into laughter.

"That's so cute," Cadwyn said. "You think people lock their doors around here. Did you not notice how easy it was to get in?"

It bothered Ozzie that, once again, Basheba knew exactly where she was going. She had no problem finding the back door that opened up to the basement, or the light switch inconveniently placed a few steps downs.

The stench of chemicals wafted out. It was only faint traces, but it burned his nose and lodged in his throat like sharp stones. He reeled back, smacking into Cadwyn who was hurriedly snuffing out his cigarette in a nearby pot plant.

"What is that?" Mina asked, one hand gently covering her nose.

"Formaldehyde," Cadwyn said. "The sweet rotten apple undertone is most likely glutaraldehyde."

"I'm failing chemistry," Ozzie said.

Burying his cigarette butt under a handful of potting soil, he elaborated simply. "Embalming fluids. Highly flammable embalming fluids. That we shouldn't be able to smell so strongly from up here."

The last sentence was directed at Basheba. Still standing a few paces down the staircase, she hesitantly turned to look at him, like she didn't want to turn her back on the stark white tiles lining the walls of the basement. Ozzie clamped a hand over his nose and pushed closer.

It wasn't hard to look over her shoulder. The lower floor looked exactly how Ozzie had imagined. Sterile and clean, with metal surfaces that gleamed under the harsh glare of the overhead lights. He tried not to look at the array of scalpels and bone saws arranged on the table. *Why do they have a microwave? What are they cooking?*

He could barely catch sight of the far wall, the one pressed up against the graveyard. The vast amount of sunlight promised there was a window there, but all he could see were rows of heavy metal shelving crammed with bottles. A single silver table stood in the middle of the room. It was empty.

Ozzie barely stifled his yelp when Cadwyn latched onto his arm and roughly yanked him back, throwing him against the opposite wall. Before he could understand what had just happened, Mina was slammed against his chest, forcing the air from his lungs. Cadwyn braced one arm against the doorframe as he reached for the short blonde.

Buck's attention was locked onto something unseen down the stairs. Shoulders hunched and teeth bared. Basheba turned. There was just enough time to see the fear in her eyes before the door slammed shut.

Chapter 12

The fluorescent lights buzzed like hornets as they flickered. Basheba pushed herself back against the door, feeling the wood rattle as Cadwyn fought to open it. She assumed it was Cadwyn. *The other two have no reason to bother.* Buck's claws scratched at the stairs as he staggered back and forth, desperate to attack, but awaiting her command. Rattling metal hinted at movement below. Something large and unseen.

"Basheba!" Cadwyn screamed.

Her hands began to shake, her heart picking up pace until she could barely breathe around it.

"Basheba!"

The scrape of flesh on tile drew closer. Shadows moved and merged as something lumbered ever closer to the bottom of the stairs.

"What's going on?" Cadwyn bellowed before striking the door in anger. "Talk to me!"

Darkness engulfed the foot of the stairs. A wall of shadows that only slightly dissipated in the staggered light. The thick body of the minotaur blocked the entire width of the stairs. It dwarfed her. Thick bands of muscles covered its chest, swelling with every snorted breath.

Most of the damage was to its skull. Spikes of bone protruded through matted tufts of fur, severing the flesh and leaving it to hang in strips. One horn still protruded proudly from its temple while the other was twisted back to resemble a goat. An eye dangled alongside its mangled snout, twisting in its steaming breath.

Basheba pressed harder against the door but there was nowhere to retreat to. The minotaur took a step closer.

"Get them out," Basheba stammered.

Cadwyn instantly replied, "What?"

Buck's snarls turned wild and savage, a ferocious sound that she felt down to her bone marrow. Basheba balled her fists until her arms trembled and her knuckles threatened to pop. She tried to draw in a deep breath and found herself choking on the chemical stench.

"Get them out!" she bellowed.

Cadwyn paused, slammed against the door again, and shouted back, "Stay away from the chemicals, Basheba!"

The sentence would have made her laugh if the scent of formaldehyde wasn't lodged like a dagger in her throat.

Will it kill me?

On the other side of the immovable wood, she could catch traces of movement; mumbled words she couldn't understand and pattering feet.

They're gone. I'm alone.

She had asked for it, and yet, the reality gutted her. The first bitter sob forced her to double over, one hand pressing tight against her stomach as if to keep everything from spilling out. Buck raged as the bull staggered forward, taking its first step onto the staircase.

Amongst the chaos, the sound of the music box rang out, filling her ears and leaving her cold. Decades of hate rose up to meet the sound, filling her with a visceral rage that left her trembling.

"Buck." Her whisper silenced the dog. It waited for her command. Glaring at the deformed face of the bull, she spoke one word. "Kill."

Nails slashed over timber as the colossal dog burst into motion. Halfway down, he launched himself at the monstrosity, wide jaws seeking flesh. The bull-man swung out a thick arm. But it underestimated both Buck's agility and his ferociousness.

Taking the blow to his torso, Buck twisted around and latched onto the beast's arm. Blood gushed from between his fangs. Bones cracked and flesh tore into strips. The minotaur thrashed and jerked in a desperate attempt to dislodge the Rottweiler.

Basheba ran for the small gap between the colossal beast and the wall. It was barely anything, but her tiny form didn't need much. The minotaur twisted just as she threaded herself through. Pain exploded across her back as a mammoth arm struck her spine and sent her careening through the air. She didn't have time to suck in a breath before she hit the far wall. Medical tools scattered around her as gravity dumped her on the bench. Sparks raced along her veins, exploding behind her eyes and whiting out her vision. A pained yelp made her head snap up.

Built from dense muscle, Buck weighed far more than she did. He flew through the air as a dark blur but landed short of the wall, sliding the rest of the distance to the side of the cabinet. No sooner had he hit the floor than he was up again, shaking blood from his muzzle, baring his fangs as he attacked.

The minotaur bellowed in fury and charged forward, trying to catch Buck with hand and horn. The dog evaded each attack, circled the beast, snapping and snarling for the minotaur's neck. The sight pushed Basheba into action. She scrambled off of the bench and snatched up a scalpel. A small plastic sheath protected her fingers from the razor tip.

Now that she was on level with the beast, its size was overwhelming. It was three times her height, broader than her entire length.

She dropped to the ground, uncapping the scalpel as she rolled under the examination table in the center of the room. It only took a few seconds for an opportunity to present itself. Basheba lashed out from her hiding place, one hand cupping the front of the humanoid shin while she raked the deadly tip across the back of its ankle. The Achilles tendon snapped with a sudden gush of blood and an agonized wail.

Basheba flung herself back under the table. Buck roared. Blood slicked the tiles. Metal squealed and crumbled as the minotaur stuck the top of the table.

Tiles turned to shrapnel under the twisted metal. Basheba scurried back, barely getting a foot away before the minotaur grabbed the edge of the table and ripped it back. Fear locked her joints. She couldn't move as the mutilated, mammoth creature loomed over her.

Buck surged forward, exploiting the distraction to leap off the exposed underside of the table and latch onto the minotaur's throat. His paws dangled as the beast staggered back. Basheba didn't know if it was the added weight, the sudden attack, or the snapped tendon, but the result was the same. The minotaur buckled. The ground shook as it dropped onto its knees. Buck thrashed his head, opening the wound and turning everything crimson.

It'll get his arms around Buck.

The thought propelled her up. A few steps and she was at the metal rack. Chemical bottles filled the shelves with a narrow window clearly intended for ventilation mounted in the wall above it. Bottles toppled as Basheba scaled the shelving. One hand shoved open the window the minotaur must have closed. Fresh air rushed in, its touch making her remember the steady burn in her lungs.

She jumped back down and scanned the shelf. *Formaldehyde.* With the heavy plastic bottle in one hand and the scalpel in the other, she sprinted back to the dueling animals. It had just gathered enough sense in its mangled mind to reach for the Rottweiler as she approached.

"Buck!" she commanded in a rush. "Release!"

Instantly, he let go. Without his grip, he dropped, narrowly avoiding the minotaur's groping hands.

The side of the scalpel pressed against the palm of her hand as she latched onto the twisted goat horn. Yanking hard, she tried to knock it off balance and buy herself another few seconds. But, with a wet, sucking sound, the horn ripped free of the scalp.

The monstrosity bellowed and struck blindly. Retreating, Basheba called for her dog and thrust a trembling hand to the window.

"Up."

He obediently bolted for the window, leaping from one shelf to the next until he could work his body through the gap. Once outside, he spun around and resumed barking, calling for her to follow. Gathering the last of her courage, Basheba held the bottle between both hands and drove it down upon the remaining horn with all of her strength.

The tip easily pierced the bottom of the bottle. A glug of liquid burst out and the air became unbreathable. She gagged and sputtered, her eyes watering and the skin around her nose burning. It looked like water. It burned like acid.

The bull-man's scream shook the walls. It was a broken, animalistic, tortured wail that twisted up her gut. The outburst of pain wasn't enough to quell the fire burning in her veins. She wiggled the bottle to widen the hole, leaping back to avoid the increased flow. There was no escaping the fumes.

Holding her breath rather than fighting for it, she darted around the flailing arms of the melting minotaur and sprinted for the bench. Without pause, she tossed the scalpel into the microwave and set the dial. It wasn't until she hit 'start' that she realized she had no idea how long it would take for the sparks to start.

Panic made her run faster than she ever thought possible. The shelves rattled wildly as she scrambled up, wiggling the bolts that attached it to the wall until the concrete chipped away. She clung to the window's edge as the shelving toppled from under her feet. Buck latched onto the back of her shirt, dragging her faster than she could crawl.

"Run!" Basheba's scream was broken by hacks and coughs. She could barely breathe.

Forcing herself up onto all fours, she was finally able to get her feet under her.

"Run!"

Through the tangle of her hair, she spotted Cadwyn and the others rounding the building. She could tell the exact moment that he caught the stench of mixing chemicals.

"Up the hill!" he bellowed, waving his arms to urge the gathering tourists to back up.

None of them listened. She didn't bother to stick around and explain. Weaving through the first thin layer of onlookers, she followed Cadwyn's advice and set her gaze on the crest.

Two more failed attempts to get people to move and Cadwyn decided to switch tactics.

"Toxic gas!"

His words incited panic. The flames that spewed from the windows of the building like it was the pits of hell caused a stampede. Explosions ripped the funeral home apart, creating fiery comets that rained down upon them. Black smoke billowed up from the points of impact, blurring her vision, leaving her unable to see the headstones before she was inches from them.

Weaving around the camouflaged obelisks and bashing into people, Basheba lost track of everyone around her. Heat filled the air as the inferno built upon itself, fed itself, grew into lapping flames that yearned to spread to the neighboring woods and shake the ground with new blasts. The hill seemed insurmountable until she broke free of the lingering smoke and the peak came into sight.

Her legs grew heavier with every step. Fire rippled down her throat and her eyes felt like embers. There wasn't anything left within her when she reached the top of the hill. She dropped, propping herself up against the nearest headstone, and tried to steady her breathing.

I just need enough to whistle. Buck will come when I whistle.

Each attempt turned into ragged coughs.

"Basheba," Cadwyn said as he dropped to one knee beside her. "Didn't I say to leave the chemicals alone? I distinctly remember telling you to leave the damned chemicals alone."

"I knew I forgot something," Basheba croaked.

She flinched as he placed a small plastic dome over her nose and mouth, pulling the attached elastic back to keep it in place. *Oxygen tank*, she realized as breathing became easier. *He comes prepared.*

"Buck," she whispered.

"I'll get your dog in a second," he said. "Just stay still."

Basheba didn't see Mina but heard her clearly over the crush of noise around her. "You set it on fire."

"You are clever," Basheba said, suddenly too tired to keep her head up.

She dropped her head back against the cool gravestone and surveyed the chaos around her. Some people screamed, grasping at fresh wounds, while even more stood in shock. Beside her, a man with an accent she couldn't place was trying to gather people to go back down and fight the flames. In a clean leap, Cadwyn stood on the rounded top of a gravestone.

"Shut up!"

He roared the words, filled them with such authority the crowd quieted down to listen. Thrusting his bright red medical bag up over his head, he continued.

"Does everyone see the medical seal? That means I'm in charge! No one is to go down the hill!"

"We have to put the fire out," the accented man argued.

Cadwyn was having none of it. "That's a funeral parlor. It's chock full of corrosive chemicals that create poisonous gas. Here, we are upwind and have clean air flow. Down there, the fumes will either kill you, or help you develop a lot of cancer later in life."

The group shuffled anxiously but didn't speak of going down again. Softening his tone, Cadwyn continued.

"I need all the able-bodied people I can get to help me tend to the wounded." He crouched down and placed a hand on the man's shoulder. "Help me. Please."

Basheba couldn't understand how the forced contact actually calmed the man down. But that, matched with Cadwyn's beseeching gaze, was enough to get the entire group of men to agree. Straightening once more, he allotted tasks to the tour guides. The first was to call the police and the other the fire department. Both of them had strict instructions to explain the dangers of the fire.

"Hands up if you're a local!" He gave them a second to comply. "Call your family, your friends, that weird neighbor. Every number you have. Tell them all to get downwind. As far north as they can. Get in a house and keep all the doors and windows closed. Make sure to tell them to take their pets and any children they're particularly fond of."

Basheba watched with no small sense of awe as the crowd obeyed his commands.

"Everyone else, we're going to set up a triage. Anyone who's wounded but conscious goes by the Leanna Winthrop grave. Head injuries by Rebecca Bell. Anyone unconscious we're going to move above the gas line. Work together. Be gentle. Then have someone sit next to them and put a hand up. I'll come as soon as I can. Oh, and if anyone with minimal injuries gets in my way demanding immediate treatment, I will make sure you never feel pain again. Understood? Okay, let's do this."

He jumped down and, before setting to his tasks, grabbed Ozzie by the front of his shirt. "Stick close to me."

"Yes, sir," Ozzie nodded without hesitation.

Bag gripped tight, Cadwyn stalked away, throwing the order over his shoulder. "Mina, take care of Basheba."

Mina stammered but slumped down on the damp earth. After a long moment, she shook her head and muttered.

"You set the place on fire."

Basheba pulled the mask back enough to mutter, "Yeah, I know."

Mina made no attempt to smother her scoff and Basheba didn't bother pretending to care. Taking as deep a breath as she was capable of, she pursed her lips and blew. Still no whistle.

"And the minotaur?" Mina asked abruptly.

"I doubt it got out."

"Convenient."

"Not really. I almost died, you know."

Finally, she was able to force a weak but full whistle. She held her breath until she heard the answering bark. An instant later, Buck was licking her face, leaving smears of minotaur blood as he tried to crawl onto her lap.

"You're not going to get away with this," Mina noted. "Destruction of property, arson, releasing poisonous chemicals in a residential neighborhood. All of it with witnesses. You're getting arrested. You know that, right?"

She chuckled, "Okay, Mina. Sure thing."

"Do you really think you're this untouchable? That a whole town will turn a blind eye?"

Smiling bitterly, Basheba rested her chin atop Buck's head. "Welcome to Black River. Where no one locks up the human sacrifices."

Chapter 13

Madness or mass corruption? The question had kept Mina up all night. Even now, as the four families overwhelmed the small parking lot, it replayed in her mind. She couldn't understand how Basheba had been allowed to walk free after what she had done. But no one had cared. At most, she had been chastised like a child and sent on her way. Leaning against the side of her father's rental car, Mina examined her memories again, searching for any hint of an answer.

Black River's fire department was astounding. They had swarmed over the burning funeral home in moments, their top of the line gas protection masks reflecting the dancing flames. Organized, well-funded, and highly trained, there hadn't been a moment of hesitation. They instantly knew what to do with the chemical fire, and they all played their parts to perfection. The building was lost, but the flames hadn't spread to the woods mere feet away.

Not exactly a volunteer rural service, she thought, one finger absently tapping against the music box in her hand. Glancing around at the dense forest surrounding the parking lot, she thought she probably shouldn't have made that assumption. *One burst of wildfire would wipe this place off the map.*

It seemed particularly unfair Basheba had escaped with fewer injuries than a lot of the innocent bystanders. The burning shrapnel that had rained down upon them had left many with broken bones and third-degree burns.

Evacuating the worst cases to the nearest town with a hospital hadn't done much to lessen the demands on Cadwyn and the local doctor. It hadn't taken long for Mina to insist she switch tasks with

Ozzie. In part, because she couldn't stand the utter indifference Basheba had for the misery she had caused. Mostly, however, she didn't want to let such an opportunity slip away.

It wasn't often an aspiring medical student could have such practical experience. On that hillside, she had learned Cadwyn was brilliant at what he did, Ozzie had the weakest stomach she had ever seen, and Basheba was most likely a sociopath.

It was hours of blood, bone, and misery.

She had never felt such a sense of purpose.

The memories brought the emotion back and she found herself smiling. Whatever traces of doubt she had still carried about her future had been obliterated. She was going to be a doctor.

Have to get through this first.

Lifting her gaze, she watched as the members of the four families continued to trickle into the tiny parking lot.

There wasn't enough room to accommodate them all. Most had been forced to leave their cars along the single narrow street that had brought them there. Kids scrambled over the remaining vehicles like ants while the adults talked amongst themselves. Tension still filled the air, but it was nothing compared to the sheer panic they had brought to the graveyard.

But it wasn't the explosion that bothered them, Mina recalled. They had been terrified one of the Selected had been killed. It begged the question; *what do they think will happen if the Witch's chosen ones die before entering the woods?*

Mina carefully stowed the thought away for later examination. Right now, she needed to understand how an entire town could experience something like that and not care. It went against all logic that Basheba was here with them, casually rechecking her camping supplies, and not in a holding cell.

Basheba had a skill for knowing when she was being watched. The moment Mina fixed her gaze on her, the blonde looked up and met her eyes. Just as quickly, she dismissed her and went back to rearranging the contents of her bag.

Mina bristled, infuriated by the brush-off and disgusted by the way the blonde continued to treat her family. Basheba's uncle had been trying to talk to his niece since they had arrived. Two hours later and Basheba had yet to say a word in response. She just walked away, leaving the little aging man to follow behind.

He keeps trying, Mina thought. *No matter how many times he's rejected, he never gives up on her. It's more than she deserves.*

"You'll be okay," Mina's mother said for the hundredth time that morning. She pulled her once more into a tight hug, pulling back only to cup Mina's cheeks with both hands. "Listen to Cadwyn. Keep him close."

"I'm so sorry." That had become her father's mantra. Something he repeated while refusing to look her in the eyes. This was the first time in her life he had failed to keep a promise to her and the shame of it seemed to weigh on his shoulders.

"It's all right, dad. Everything will be fine, you'll see."

"I should have got you out of this. I should have found a way."

We could just leave. She didn't dare voice the words. Family pressures and tradition were hard things to break.

You don't have to fix it. I will.

She wouldn't admit it to anyone, but there had been moments in the past few days when doubt had started to build up. *Pebbles of doubt can build a battlement if you let it.*

Being here didn't help. There was just something about the ancient woods that made her uneasy. Seeing her strong, proud parents broken like this did more to dispel her fears than any reassurances could have. Their tears hardened her resolve to end the charade.

Prove the hoax and set them free from this insanity.

"I'll be fine, really," Mina insisted, squeezing her mother's shoulders once more.

"Don't underestimate the Witch Woods," her father warned. "It's a dangerous place."

"I think I'm taking the greater danger with me," Mina mumbled, barely able to keep her gaze from darting over to Basheba. She wasn't sure how she felt about sharing a tent with a girl who played with her dog as people burned.

Her father's quizzical expression broke into a boastful smile. "That's the attitude, darling. Give her hell. But come back to us."

"I will."

Her mother's hand grasped her wrist, squeezing until Mina gasped in pain.

"Mom?"

"You have to come back."

"I will. I promise."

Lowering her voice to a whisper, her mother met her gaze with an unblinking stare. "You must come back. Do whatever you have to. But come back."

Nails dug through the layers of Mina's jacket to reach her skin. The small spike of pain made her mother's meaning clear. *Whatever* it takes.

"It won't come to that," Mina insisted as she pulled her arm free and forced a smile. "We'll work together."

"The Witch can take the rest of them. But not you. Give her what she wants, you have the stomach for it, I know it."

Mina glanced to her father for help but found only a matching conviction.

"I'm not going to hurt anyone," Mina said.

"They don't have to suffer. Make it quick. In the bottom of your bag, there's a container of belladonna leaves. You only need one leaf for each person. Put it in their food. It'll be over before they know it."

Mina's skin went cold. Her blood stopped flowing in her veins, and the earth crumbled from under her feet.

"I'm not a murderer."

The words passed her lips as a whisper. She was afraid to say it out loud. Terrified to confirm that the woman who had raised her with gentle hands and kind words had just ordered her to kill.

"Listen to your mother."

The weakness was gone from her father's voice, replaced with something dark and cold. Mina didn't have time to pull back. Someone unseen blew a horn, making the entire crowd fall into a tense silence. One more long bellow of the Viking-like horn and Mina noticed Cadwyn cutting through the crowd. He smiled and waved to his weeping family until he stood before the man with the horn. Basheba and Buck joined them on the little patch of grass that separated the parking lot from the start of the hiking trail.

"You have to go now," her mother said. "Remember what I told you."

Mina nodded. In her shock, she was barely able to mumble, "I love you."

Turning, she was captured by Jeremiah's arms. He hugged her until she couldn't breathe.

"I'll walk with you," he whispered.

The walk itself was too surreal for Mina's brain to understand. Everything came in small pieces unrelated to the others. The crunch of gravel under her feet. Whispered well wishes as the crowd parted before her. The weight of her camping bag. Sun-warmed skin and the morning dew sinking into the hem of her jeans. Within a blink, Jeremiah had fallen away, and she was standing next to Ozzie. She looked over her shoulder to find her brother again.

With the same disorientation, she followed Cadwyn and the others into the woods. The trees welcomed them with outstretched arms, quickly shielding them from the morning sun and shrouding them in a damp chill. The trail twisted rapidly, sharp turns that weaved around the thickest of the old growth and quickly cut them off from the rest of the world. The rising sunlight made the leaves glow. Birds fluttered about overhead, preparing for the coming cold and a cluster of squirrels chased each other across the path before them. A lazy stream, unseen but heard, bubbled past to stir the silence.

"Did that man have a Viking horn?" The question cracked out of Mina before she realized she had formed it.

Cadwyn shrugged. "It's tradition."

"How?"

Her question overlapped Ozzie's own.

"This is actually kind of nice. Is the whole walk like this?"

Both Ozzie and Mina turned to Cadwyn for a response. He looked to Basheba, wordlessly reminding them both that this was his first time as well. Refusing to pause for the conversation, she took the lead, Buck trotting by her feet. The dog had been outfitted with a backpack of his own and Mina was struck with the sudden curiosity to know what was in it.

"We're not in the Witch's Woods yet."

"Huh?" Ozzie said.

"A nature preserve butts up against the Witch's Woods," she explained. "We're just cutting through here so we can stay out of her territory for as long as possible."

"So, when exactly will we cross over?" Mina asked.

"You'll know."

With that, Basheba settled back into silence. It didn't matter what the rest of them discussed, she refused to engage, only acknowledging the presence of her dog.

They started at dawn and paused for lunch at noon. Already, Ozzie's new boots were making his heels blister. Cadwyn tended to them and rearranged the bags between the four of them, trying to lighten the boy's load. Mina's stomach had squirmed as he had riffled through her pack, sure he was going to discover the poison her mother had supposedly given her. Despite her best efforts, he still noticed her relief when he handed the pack back. In a small mercy, he mistook it and smiled.

"It'll be a bit lighter for you. Let me know if you need me to change it around again."

Mina said she would, but she knew she wouldn't, not until Basheba showed any sign of discomfort. Mina hated the fact that the smallest, weakest one amongst them was struggling the least.

Three more hours of hiking, and she started noticing the warning signs nailed into the trees that lined the path. *No trespassing. Turn back. Do not enter.*

"Should we be walking here?" Ozzie asked. "Maybe we took a wrong turn."

"We're just off the Witch's Woods. The police put them up to try and deter people from entering," Basheba replied.

Mina eyed the next sign she passed, a brightly colored one that urged the reader to turn back and had a suicide hotline scrawled across the bottom. A chuckle escaped her lips unbidden.

"What is with this town? If they really think the Witch is a threat, why don't they do anything about it?"

Basheba pointed to a nearby sign as she stalked past it.

"Signs? That's the best they can do?"

"What exactly do you want them to do?" Basheba countered. "Arrest her for being an illegal witch?"

"Haunting without a license?" Cadwyn offered with a small smile.

"Maybe they could do an exorcism," Ozzie suggested. "You know, bless the woods and force her out."

"They tried that when this first became a problem," Cadwyn said.

Basheba snorted, finally stopping and calling Buck over. "It's not their problem."

"Of course," Mina said. "Why on earth would they care about people dying?"

She had known Basheba would reply quickly but hadn't been prepared for her response.

"The harvest."

"I'm sorry, what?"

"Haven't you noticed that for a nothing little town, this place looks really good? Nice cars. Nicer houses. Nothing that should be within their budgets. Pick any farm at random, and you'll find it brimming with produce. Not just produce. *Perfect* produce. Walk through an orchard, and you won't find a single apple that's misshapen or rotten."

Mina blinked. "The Witch bribes the townsfolk with plentiful harvests?"

"Yeah. I think she does."

Again, Mina didn't mean to laugh. It just came out. "That's what you meant about human sacrifices? What are they? Ancient pagans?"

"Sure. Because they're the only people ever, in the history of the world, to think human sacrifice was a good idea," Basheba deadpanned. "And no one ever does anything monstrous for personal gain or a belief in the greater good."

"The whole town is pretty obsessed with the Witch," Ozzie mumbled.

"And Roswell is obsessed with aliens. That doesn't mean they exist."

"I'm confused. Are you saying Katrina is a real threat and the police should intervene? Or that she's just a local legend and not worth anyone's time?"

Mina found herself staring at Basheba, unable to answer.

"Well, this has been productive," Cadwyn cut in. "How about we have a look at the map?"

Basheba pulled the map from her pocket, unfolding it as she knelt down. Cadwyn helped her trap the edges under small rocks to keep the wind from taking it. Yellow highlighter marks pointed out the essential places; where they came in, where they'll turn off, the far off point that Mina assumed was their destination. Ozzie wasn't afraid to ask questions and had Basheba explain each one.

"What's this place?" Mina asked, pointing to the line of pink dots that arched between the yellow marks.

"Potential campsites," Basheba said.

"And these two black marks?"

Tension filled Basheba's shoulders. "Two things I was hoping to avoid. Unfortunately, we're running too far behind. We're going to have to cut between the two of them."

"But what are they?" Mina asked.

Cadwyn leaned forward to tap one of the marks. "I know that one's the Devil's Tree, right?"

"What's the Devil's Tree?" Ozzie asked.

"It's the tree they used to hang people from," Mina said. "My grandma used to tell me legends about it. Apparently, it's cursed. If you get too close, the ghosts will grab you and lynch you up with them."

"Yet another thing you're too smart to believe?" Basheba muttered.

"I have no doubt horrible things happened there, and that it was used as a suicide spot for many people. That doesn't make it supernatural."

Basheba grunted.

"I would ask you for evidence, but you tend to set that on fire," Mina added.

"What's this one?" Ozzie blurted, the words clashing together in his haste to get them out.

He shot nervous looks around the group before Basheba answered in a flat tone.

"Bell's Brook."

"Your family found it?" Ozzie asked, clearly hopeful for a conversation change.

Basheba smiled, her eyes dead and cold. "My namesake drowned in it."

Ozzie instantly deflated and stammered out an apology.

"How were you to know?" Basheba dismissed, busying herself with the pockets of Buck's saddlebags.

"Bare bones history," Cadwyn cut in. "Basheba Senior was gathering berries with her friends. She went to cross the brook and fell in. After laughing for a bit, her friends realized she hadn't come up and waded out to help her. It was then they discovered the brook was only three inches deep where she disappeared. Her body was never found."

"I don't go near that water."

Basheba spat the words out as she finished fastening the last belt of Buck's new harness. He still carried the saddlebags, but now they sat upon armor instead of fur. The thick harness covered his chest and spine with sharp two-inch spikes. With a matching collar and what could be best described as a tactical dog helmet, he looked ready for war.

"Where did you even get that?" Mina mumbled without thinking.

"Same place I got these."

Basheba tossed a small bag to each of them. A collar and twin cuffs of the same make were inside. It didn't click in Mina's head until she saw both Basheba and Cadwyn putting theirs on.

"You want us to wear these?"

"They protect your most exposed arteries. Neck and wrists. Also keeps people from choking you." Cadwyn ended with a warm smile and a passing, "It's tradition."

Once everyone was outfitted and Basheba had safely tucked the map away, they swooped under the metal bar that separated the main trail from the Witch's Wood.

For the first hour, everything remained the same—a crisp autumn day with all the beauty a day like that could hold. During the second, things changed. It started gradually, so Mina didn't notice at first. A dulling of color, a dip in temperature, a thickening of trees. The mist lacked such subtlety. Mina watched in shock as it rolled toward them as a wave, swooping around the tree trunks and leaving a thin layer of frost upon everything it touched.

None of them managed to smother their gasped cries. First contact was like submerging their feet in ice water. Numbing to the point where it almost felt like fire. A thousand needles driving through her boots to find her flesh.

"I hate this stuff," Basheba muttered, pausing to angrily rip open one of the pockets of Buck's bag. Again, she brought enough for everyone.

Mina caught hers with both hands. "Feet warmers?"

"They start working upon contact with air," Basheba said. "Put them in your boots. They're horrible to walk on, but you won't get frostbite."

As Mina ripped open the pack, she heard Basheba add in a whisper. "Hopefully."

"This happened to you before?" Ozzie asked as he hopped around, unwilling to sit in the airborne frost to put on his shoes.

"It's part of her game."

Ozzie stopped, growing motionless as a weak smile curled his full lips. "I'm really glad you're here with me."

For a moment, Basheba was held in stunned silence, staring at him like a deer caught in a car's headlights.

"Sure," she said at last. "Don't mention it."

Cadwyn straightened his spine, drawing himself up to his full height to look around. Distracted by the conversation and the cold, Mina had missed the greater implications of the fog. It covered the path. And, without it, she was lost. The dense trees all looked the same. The more she looked, the less she saw, until nothing looked real anymore.

"Basheba?" Cadwyn said, pulling a compass from his pocket as he inched closer.

She waited until she had put little socks on Buck's feet before retrieving the map from her back pocket. The instant it was free, the dog reared up. It latched onto the paper and ripped it from her hands. A sudden breeze claimed it before Basheba could snatch it back. The paper flapped, toppled, and danced on the air, weaving through the bare branches and luring them further from the path. They all knew it. But the need for the map forced their hand.

Running until sweat dripped down her spine, Mina lunged for the paper. It spiraled around her arm, staying just beyond the reach of her fingers, before soaring higher. Lunging after it, she burst into a barren meadow.

The grass was brown and brittle, crumbling with the slightest amount of pressure. It was the first time since dawn she had been able to glimpse the sky. The clear blue was gone, choked behind heavy clouds that pressed down upon the canopy. A single gnarled tree stood in the middle of the dead earth. Swollen and bare and formed like a hand reaching toward the sky. Mina heard the others join her but didn't look at them.

"I take it that's the Devil's Tree," she whispered.

Cadwyn nodded.

"Up there!" Ozzie's outburst made everyone turn to him before they realized he was pointing to the top of the tree. Tangled around the highest branch, the map flapped like a flag.

Relief bloomed behind Mina's ribs, barely stifled by the weary expressions the others wore. She stripped off her pack and placed it at Ozzie's feet.

"Cadwyn, can you give me a boost please?"

His eyes widened.

"It's lucky for all of us I'm a good climber," she smiled.

Basheba stepped closer, "You don't have to. We have the compass."

"Yeah, you're not the least bit convincing."

She flinched back. "Did anyone else bring a map?"

"This is mostly stuff Ozzie bought me," Cadwyn said.

It was the same story for all of them. Frustration brewed on Basheba's face until she bit savagely at her lips.

"I should have bought more than one. It was stupid of me. I meant to get more yesterday."

"It's okay, Basheba. I'll just go get it." When soothing didn't work, she added somewhat playfully, "Yell if anything weird comes close."

The group cautiously edged closer to the tree. Cadwyn braced his back against the trunk and cupped his hands, transforming himself into a human ladder. Grabbing his shoulders helped her to balance.

"This is a trap, you know," he whispered. After a moment's pause, he added, "If anything happens, jump. I'll catch you."

"Thanks," she said, because she felt like she should respond, but didn't know what else to say.

One firm push and an awkward stomp on his shoulders allowed her to reach the lowest branch. She scrambled up, her new hiking boots scrapping away the bark. Focus was her strong suit. She used it now, fixing her attention on the map, surging toward it, letting everything else fade away.

Branches thinned as she got higher. Some cracked and threatened to snap under her weight. Higher and higher, until she was straining, her fingers trembling and her shoulder threatening to pop from its socket. One final surge and the paper was in her grasp. Her landing broke the branch. It crashed down to the earth as she scrambled to keep from following. How she managed it, she had no idea, but she ended up swinging around the trunk and landing hard on another, far sturdier branch.

"Mina?" Cadwyn called.

Pressing her forehead against the trunk, she thrust her hand out. "I've got it."

As she straightened herself, she heard it. A low, steady buzz. Shifting and living and swarming. *Bees.* Her heart skipped a beat and jammed itself into her throat. The map ripped on the bark as she grasped the tree with both hands, trying to hold her panic at bay.

"Cadwyn?" It came out as a whisper. She cleared her throat and tried again. "Cadwyn?"

"I'm right here. Right under you. Just fall back."

"Where's the hive?" *He must see them. That's why he sounds like that. God, they're so loud.*

"Listen to me, Mina," Basheba said. "Close your eyes and fall to the left. We'll catch you, okay? Just close your eyes and fall."

Just tell me where the hive is!

"Mina! Just do what I'm telling you!"

Her body reacted to the direct order, but not in compliance. Twisting her head to the right, she forced her eyes open. There, dangling from the nearby branch, she found the hive. Fat insects of black and yellow squirmed and swarmed. Crawling over each other as they delved into the honeycomb labyrinth they had created in the hollowed-out eye socket. The hanged man dangled from his noose, decayed and bloated, riddled with bees as they burrowed under his flesh to create their home.

"Mina!" Cadwyn roared.

A scream ripped out of her chest. The corpse twisted, swaying as the bees burst free from his body, their numbers blacking out the sun.

Chapter 14

The Devil's Tree convulsed violently, lurching from side to side. Half frozen clumps of earth hurled out in every direction as the roots ripped free of the soil. What started as a slight hum confined to the open, dangling corpse grew to a deafening roar. He could barely hear himself as he screamed for Mina to jump. Stubborn to the end, the girl hadn't listened. She had looked.

"Jump, Mina!"

Her answering scream came with a thunderous crack of splintering wood. The top branches exploded, releasing a wild swarm that blanketed the sky. A wall of stinging insects hid her from his view.

Cadwyn braced himself to catch her, but the impact didn't come instantly. The droning hive covered any sound that might have given him a hint of where she was. They rushed at the group, raining down upon them like fire. He could feel the bees' venom swell under his skin. Grinding his teeth against the pain, he forced his arms to remain outstretched, waiting. She still hadn't come down.

The tree rattled. Thick branches dropped through the living cloud, slamming into the earth and making it tremble. Mina's scream almost went unnoticed. He shifted toward it at the last moment. The impact sent them both sprawling across the brittle earth. Mina's elbow drove into his mouth and blood splashed his tongue. He didn't know which one of them it belonged to. Rolling to the side as best he could, he tried to bundle the frantic girl close, tried to shield her from the attack. The insects went straight for their eyes, their mouths, crawled under the necklines of their shirts in a hunt for tender flesh.

"Up!"

Bees crawled over his lips, trying to squirm down his throat, piercing his gums and tongue. Cadwyn swiped at his mouth and spat, attempting to clear his airway.

But there were always more.

A thousand needles stabbed him all at once and flooded his bloodstream with venom. Trembling with pain, he looped an arm around Mina's waist and dragged her to her feet. Mina kicked and screamed, too far beyond the point of reason to even try to calm down. He swooped low, tossed her over his throbbing shoulder, and sprinted across the open field.

Breaking free from the heart of the swarm and clawing at his eyes, he was able to catch a few fleeting glimpses of the others. Basheba had haphazardly wrapped her thick knitted scarf around her head to leave only her eyes exposed. It did little to keep the insects at bay. Running didn't dislodge the layer of bright yellow and black that covered her arms.

She latched onto Ozzie's shoulder with one tiny hand and kicked hard at the back of his knee, driving him to the ground. He fought the touch until she yanked his scarf up over his head to bring him some small measure of relief.

"To the woods!" Basheba bellowed.

The dead earth crumbled under their feet as they stampeded for the tree line, revealing tangled roots and potholes to catch them. Half blind, Cadwyn ran until he felt the sharp twigs slash across his face and rip at his arms. Pain radiated from the stings to mask any damage the plant life caused. He kept running, trying to keep Basheba and Ozzie in sight through squinted eyes, unable to leave the swarm behind completely.

Each insect he knocked aside was replaced by a dozen more. Shrubs and fallen trees caught his legs. Coupled with Mina's constantly shifting weight dragging down one shoulder, he stumbled and tripped. The pain was the only thing that kept him moving. Pain, and the simple plan to follow Basheba's retreating back.

"Left!" Basheba screamed.

He jerked around obediently, following her voice until the ground gave out from under him, and he fell. It was a short drop with rocks and icy water at the end. He tried to soften the impact for Mina, twisting around to take as much of it as he could, but there was little he could do. The stones found every newly forming bruise and stoked the fire the bee venom had ignited in his skin. He cried out in agony. Bees swarmed the instant his mouth opened.

Then he hit the river's surface. Icy water flooded his mouth and sent the insects into a wild panic. He spat and choked as his throat swelled.

Cadwyn forced his head under the water, gaining a few seconds reprieve while using the current to force the insects from his mouth. He stayed until the need for air made his lungs burn. A sharp tug on his backpack jerked him back up. Blinking the water from his eyes, he flung an arm back. Bees squished between his skin and the slender wrist he latched onto.

Basheba. It's too small to be anyone else.

She wrenched her hand free of his fingers and jerked at his bag again. Only after she had found what she was looking for did it occur to him that she was trying to fight her way inside his medical pack.

A deep whoosh covered the sound of the droning hive. Blistering heat washed over him and scorched the fine hairs on his neck. He flattened himself into the water but the river wasn't deep enough to let him escape the flames. Then, just as suddenly as it began, it all faded away.

Rearing back, he gasped for air and tried to peer through his swelling eyes. His vision cleared just as Basheba turned to face him, an aerosol can of antiseptic spray in one hand and his Zippo lighter in the other. Shock coursed through him as he watched her bring the items together. The spray caught the flames and released a guttural whoosh.

She wielded the makeshift flamethrower with focused determination, systematically setting the swarm alight, turning them into burning embers that spiraled through the air and fell like ash.

Cadwyn choked on a breath as she suddenly shifted, bringing the flood of fire barreling toward him. Snapping one hand up, he gripped the back of Mina's head and forced her down into the water. There was barely any depth for her to retreat into.

Her screams bubbled and gasped as the icy stream flowed around them. His front froze while his back burned. Mina never stopped fighting him, forcing him to tighten his grip and bring her to the brink of drowning. His head was spinning and his limbs felt like lead when Basheba finally pushed the flames aside.

His arms trembled as he forced himself up onto all fours and dropped to the side, gasping for air, relishing the swell of his lungs even as his throat throbbed with agony. Mina sputtered but couldn't stop sobbing. Propping her up against his shoulder, he looked downstream, searching for Basheba again.

She stood only a few feet away. Her small chest heaved and her raw hands trembled. But her eyes blazed with focused fury as she glared toward the riverbank. Cadwyn desperately searched for Ozzie before catching sight of him around Basheba's legs. The boy was beaten, shivering, too horrified to move from his seat within the Arctic stream, but alive.

Cadwyn braced his hand on a submerged stone and rocked himself into motion. But before he could get his feet under him, he recalled that Basheba was staring something down.

A man stood on the banks. Thick and sturdy, several feet taller than Cadwyn himself. The surviving bees crawled over him, clustered into a squirming flesh of ebony and brilliant yellow. The only part of the man's actual body that was visible under the swarm was his eyes. Catlike, putrid yellow, and terrifyingly familiar.

For a split second, Cadwyn felt himself thrown back in time, back to when he was just a boy and something demonic had slithered under his brother's flesh.

It can't be the same one.

An almost humanoid shape stared them down. Waiting. Glaring at Basheba with a hatred that matched her own.

Basheba snapped her hands up. Before she could reignite the spray, she dropped. Her last act before disappearing under the surface of the water was to toss the two items she held into the air. Ozzie's shout snapped Cadwyn from his shock. The teen had thrown his entire body forward, managing to catch both the lighter and the aerosol can, keeping them in the air and sending them toward Cadwyn, leaving him no way to break his fall.

Ozzie body-slammed the jagged stones, the impact sending up a wall of water. It struck Cadwyn like liquid ice as he lunged for the items. They fumbled across his fingertips until he was able to pull them into his grasp. Holding them tight, he glanced over to find Ozzie half submerged; his head and torso lost within the sloshing water as his legs restlessly searched for a nook to lock his toes in.

A sharp drag pulled them deeper into the impossible sinkhole. Slick stones clicked against each other as they toppled out of the way, leaving Ozzie with nothing to hold onto. Cadwyn started toward them just as Mina screamed.

Whirling around, his limbs moved before his conscious mind could catch up. He released the flammable antiseptic spray and lit it. The heat of the flames pulsated against his river-numbed fingers, the glow stung his eyes, making his already limited vision ripple.

The human hive burst at the first contact with the flames, shattering apart into a million tiny insects that swept around to encase them. He raked the fire back and forth. Years of muscle memory warned him the can was becoming too light. It was going to run dry.

Ozzie reared back, his face barely breaking free of the frothing water. "Mina!"

The boy trembled with the strain it took to bring Basheba up. It took all of his strength to lift her enough for her to gasp once before the unseen force caught her again. Whatever had her, dragged her down with enough power to almost claim Ozzie as well.

Cadwyn shifted, trying to carve a clear path for Mina to reach the others. Only when Ozzie cried out again did Cadwyn realize Mina hadn't moved. He glanced over to find her where he had left her. Curled into a tight ball, she screamed and whimpered, clawing frantically at herself until blood stained the shallow pool she sat in.

"Mina! Help!" Ozzie pleaded.

Her screams became a string of nonsense.

Cadwyn looked from her to the others, and realized he was trapped. If he moved to help Ozzie, Mina would be left unprotected. If he didn't, the young boy might drown along with Basheba.

While Cadwyn hesitated, Ozzie brought one hand out of the water, bracing it on the rocks to push himself high enough to bellow.

"Buck!"

The dog didn't come to the stranger's call. Ozzie slid forward a few inches until his mouth was barely above the dark inky liquid.

"Buck!"

Cadwyn twitched with the need to run to them. He turned back to Mina, a desperate plea on his tongue. All he needed was a split second to know there was nothing he could do. Her panic attack had a tight hold on her that only time could release. Seconds passed in a blur, each one bringing him to the point of no return. If he didn't choose who to save, they were both going to die.

The swarm's drone diminished Ozzie's half-wild cry while the whoosh of fire and Mina's whimpered sobs crowded into Cadwyn's skull.

Make the call.

An abrupt bark spared him. Head low and back protected, Buck sprinted through the wall of swarming insects with single-minded determination. Reaching Ozzie's side, he barked and paced the edge of the pit. Ozzie flopped out his one free arm to try and catch the dog.

The swarm took Cadwyn's attention and, by the time he looked back, Ozzie had twisted his body around to plant his feet against the stones on either side of the pit. All his efforts barely managed to drag

Basheba up. It was more her backpack than her actual body, and he almost lost his grip when the bees clustered.

Cadwyn swung the flame around to drive off the onslaught. The brilliant glow filled his vision for an instant and, by the time it cleared, Ozzie had hooked one of Basheba's bag straps around a spike protruding from Buck's armor. A swift smack to the dog's rear sent the Rottweiler plowing forward. The soaked material snapped taut while the water frothed. A few of the stitches popped. Buck's muscles trembled. Ozzie scrambled up to help and then, just as quickly as it had begun, it all stopped.

The bees vanished. The pain they had brought lingered even as the stings dissipated. Basheba didn't shoot free from the pit. Instead, the riverbed simply returned to its original form. A shallow brook barely large enough to find her torso.

Now, without the resistance, Ozzie was flung to the ground and Buck took off at a sprint. As she coughed up a lungful of water, Basheba managed to croak out a command for him to stop. The dog's obedience was instantaneous, and she was left to flop over the sun-warmed stones.

In the sudden stillness, the heat pressing against his hands was brought to the forefront of Cadwyn's awareness. He hissed, dropped to one knee, and, after sparing a second to toss the items onto a nearby stone, he dunked his hands into the frigid water. The chaos of noise that had filled the forest was now reduced to sporadic gasped breaths, Mina's sobs, and the soft trickle of water flowing over the rocks.

Cadwyn pushed aside his confusion and brewing panic to call out. "Ozzie? Are you okay?"

"I don't know."

"Is anything broken? Can you see bone?"

There was a brief pause. "No."

"Take care of Mina."

With that, Cadwyn jumped up and ran to Basheba. The heavy waterlogged pack kept her on her back, each mouthful of water she spat up sloshing over her face. Carefully, he rolled her into a recovery position, barely able to assess the damage as Buck nuzzled her with concern. Her lips were blue, her body shook, and her chest heaved as it tried to work the icy liquid out of her lungs.

Get them somewhere warm and safe.

The simple thought played across his mind as the sun began to sink behind the dense forest and the shadows crept in.

CHAPTER 15

"But I felt them," Mina whispered to herself.

She pressed her torso against her thighs and stared at the ground before her, willing herself to concentrate, to dislodge the fog that had wrapped around her brain. *There has to be an explanation*, she told herself. *A logical explanation. I just have to think.*

The distorted face of the hanging man filled her mind's eye. She could almost smell the honey the hive had gathered within the rotting skull. Her stomach convulsed. Throwing herself to the side, she retched. Bile and spit splattered over the dead leaves.

"Really, Mina?" Basheba sighed. "In the middle of the campsite? You couldn't have walked a few feet in literally any direction?"

Her fingers shook too hard for her to wipe her mouth with any kind of dignity. *Think, Mina. Find the answer. There has to be an answer.*

The fire Basheba had started did little to fight off the gathering shadows, but it did work to ease the ice that had encased her bones. Mina had been the only one to lose her backpack. If Cadwyn hadn't had the forethought to put a thermal blanket in his med-pack, she would have been left naked with only the fire to warm her. No one had a similar size.

The looming threat of nightfall had shifted everyone's priorities. Darkness and hypothermia seemed more important than making peace with the madness they had just experienced, especially when thin snow had started to fall, gathering with the lingering mist to leave them all shivering. There was no shelter in sight. Only an endless stretch of bone-white trees and shadows. They wouldn't last the night without the sleeping bags Cadwyn had stowed in her bag when he had redistributed the weight amongst the group. So the boys had hurriedly changed into somewhat dry clothes and set off to retrieve her pack, leaving them to set up camp.

Basheba hadn't waited for them to be out of sight before she instructed Mina to just sit down and keep out of her way. There was a practiced efficiency in everything she did, a quiet confidence in how she performed her tasks. From picking the perfect location amongst the trees for the tent, to how she constructed the fire. In those few moments that Mina's mind strayed away from the problem before her, she watched Basheba.

Her first action had been to start the fire. A healthy, fat teepee of flames that reminded Mina of family bonfires. The tent had gone up almost instantaneously under her skilled manipulations, and she had been busying herself ever since with tasks Mina couldn't name. She had never really been into camping.

Mina's thoughts returned once more to all her unanswered questions and dwelled there ever since. She studied her hands. The firelight turned her skin copper. There wasn't a single welt.

"But I felt them," she mumbled.

"You know what's a fun game?" Basheba said abruptly. She sat back on her heels; forearms smeared with mud from the pit she was digging. "Silence. Let's play silence."

The words swirled in Mina's head until they fell into some kind of meaningful order.

"What are you doing?"

"Building a fire."

"We have one."

"A cooking fire," Basheba said, stocking small twigs into the pit. "Dakota holes are also good for drying clothes."

"Dakota holes?"

"Large hole for fire. Smaller hole for the chimney. Link the two with a tunnel. You get concentrated heat without exposed flames." Basheba rattled off the facts while unpeeling a few tampons she had retrieved from her pocket. Noticing Mina's glance, she smiled and wiggled them in the air. "They're great for tinder. And come in handy as waterproof packs."

She reached into the pit, her slender shoulders shifted slightly, and a bright orange glow emerged from the hole. Smiling contently, Basheba took a moment to warm her hands. It was the only time she had been still since the boys had left.

"You taught yourself all of this?"

Basheba closed her eyes and huffed. "What happened to playing the silent game?"

"Do you have a problem with me?" Mina asked.

"Several," she replied with an almost playful shrug.

Anger trickled into Mina's stomach, twisting with her fear until she had to clench her jaw to keep from screaming. Taking in a sobering breath, she schooled her features and forced her voice to come out calm.

"We should talk about that."

Basheba barked a laugh, pausing in her activity to spare her one fleeting glance.

"Why?"

"It seems important that we get along."

"We're never going to get along," the blonde replied airily, busying herself with twigs and leaves once again. "We're born to be at odds, little girl."

Mina rolled her eyes. "Why? Because two women can't work for a similar goal without a cat-fight breaking out?"

Basheba blinked at her, a smile creeping across her face. "Wow. You just full-on channeled your daddy there, didn't you?" She shrugged. "I guess the arrogant, self-righteous fruit doesn't roll far from the tree."

Mina couldn't stifle her snort. "Those are two qualities you're in no position to be accusing others of."

Basheba's smile carried all the venom her dead eyes were incapable of. Mina tightened her arms around her knees and forced herself to meet her expressionless gaze.

"You really want me to tell you why we can't get along? Because you're clearly not going to get it on your own." Feeding the submerged fire made light dance across her pale face. "We want fundamentally different things. And since we're both goal-driven, we're bound to clash. I can't get on board with your hero complex. Or the superiority one for that matter."

"Both better options than your Napoleon complex," Mina shot back.

Basheba giggled. It wasn't the reaction Mina was aiming for.

"Yeah, I suppose you have me there," she dismissed almost wistfully. "My point is that you want to save the world. You want to be the one to fling open the gates and save the poor, inept, ignorant villages from their self-imposed dark ages."

Mina squirmed but lifted her chin. "And what do you want?"

She hummed pleasantly. "If I had all the money in the world, I'd build a wall around all of Black River. A large, impenetrable wall."

"Okay." Mina frowned in confusion. It wasn't what she had been expecting.

Light danced in Basheba's eyes. "And then I'd lock the gate and set it all on fire. The town. The forest. Just sit back with a beer and watch it burn."

"What is with you and fire?"

"I don't know. I just think it's neat." Poking a stick into the concealed flames coaxed flickering embers to drift up and dance across the night sky. She watched it all with a dreamy smile. "I'd love to see how many of those fine townsfolk chose to burn with their crops. They're more than willing to see us die for them. Bet they'll have a different view on human sacrifice when they're the ones on the altar, though."

"Wait," Mina cut in as her stomach rolled. "In your fantasy, you'd locked all those people in when you burn the town?"

Utter confusion scrunched up Basheba's face. "Duh. Otherwise, what's the point?"

Is she really this twisted, or is it just a show? A self-defense mechanism?

Either way, it left a sour taste in Mina's mouth. It was the contentment in Basheba's eyes that scared her the most. The glassy, doll-like orbs finally had some life in them. Something that, until now, only Buck had managed to accomplish. But even as dread gathered inside her like a coming storm, she couldn't fight off her exhaustion. It sunk down to her bone-marrow and pulled at her eyes. She would have probably fallen asleep where she sat if it wasn't for her constant shivering. Hard, rattling shutters that left her breathless and were impossible to stop.

Mina wanted nothing more than to end the conversation. She knew now nothing good could come from long discussions with Basheba Bell. But each time she kept her silence, she felt panic sparking along the edge of her awareness. Without a distraction, she'd fall back into hysterics. Already, she could almost hear the bees again. If Basheba was her only option to keep control of her brain, she'd take it.

"Why do you hate them so much?" Mina asked.

"Really? They allowed the complete slaughter of my entire family because they were given apples, and you wonder why I don't like them?"

She's insane, Mina decided. A loud buzz passed behind her and she flinched, twisting around to study the woods.

"Did you hear that?"

"It's the woods at night," Basheba said, already working to construct a rack out of twigs. "There's a lot to hear. Care to be a tad more specific?"

Mina pulled the thermal blanket tighter around her shoulders. "Bees."

Basheba stilled and stared lifelessly in front of her. "Nope."

The silence that followed worked on Mina's nerves. She needed conversation.

"Not your entire family."

Already arranging the makeshift clothesline over the fire pit,

Basheba sighed dramatically. "I know I'm going to regret asking this, but what are you babbling about?"

"You said the town killed your *entire* family. That's not true."

"They killed all the ones who mattered," Basheba dismissed.

"Why do you hate your uncle so much?"

Basheba jabbed the rack into place and began arranging the damp clothes to dry. As calm as her body was, her face was in constant motion. Shifting rapidly between a manic smile, a furious snarl, and a tearful sob. Eventually, her features settled into a smile completely devoid of any emotion.

"Now, that's a bit personal. We haven't even braided each other's hair and talked about boys yet."

"If it's too personal, you don't have to tell me."

"Yeah. That's kind of what I was getting at. But nice try making me feel guilty about not opening up. Smooth attempt at manipulation."

"I wasn't trying to do that. I'm just trying to have an actual conversation with you. Maybe even understand you a little. Are you always this paranoid?"

Basheba smiled again, small and tight and with a bitter amusement in her eyes. "I'm not paranoid. I just don't like people. Everyone who's worth anything is dead, anyway."

"You like Cadwyn," Mina pointed out.

"He follows me on Instagram." Basheba turned to her, one delicate hand placed over her heart. "That's a sacred bond."

Frustration piled up inside her until she was teetering on the edge of screaming again.

"What happened to you to make you like this?"

All traces of humor were swept from Basheba like a flash of wildfire, leaving only smoldering embers burning in her pale blue eyes.

"It must have been nice to be so utterly protected from reality," she said slowly. "You must have known your family members were dying. What did your daddy tell you? Did he say they were in car crashes? Maybe freak accidents? You'd think that eventually, you'd get a little suspicious you weren't getting the whole story."

She didn't get louder or throw her arms about, but it was clear Basheba was fueling her anger. It was growing and bubbling inside her. Mina was suddenly very aware that she was alone in a dark forest with a volatile, unpredictable, and possibly sadistic girl.

"My earliest childhood memory is of this place," Basheba continued, abruptly taking on an almost dreamy tone. "My older sister had been selected. None of them returned. When that happens, we form search parties to find the remains. I volunteered."

"The police let you? How old were you?"

Basheba flopped back onto the earth. Apparently, rolling her eyes wasn't dramatic enough. Bathed in the dancing light of the nearby fire, she stared up at the canopy, letting the tiny flakes of snow drift onto her face.

"You're so dumb it's physically painful." Basheba chuckled. "About a century in, the Black River police admitted to themselves there wasn't much they could do. Admitting there was a killer in the woods only put pressure on them to catch said killer. So, instead of being forced to hang innocent people to prevent riots, they decided to take a step back. Sure, they'll come and take statements and photos and tick all the boxes necessary to make sure the paperwork's in order. But anything more just leads to the deaths being exploited. We become entertainment. Promote Katrina's legend. Draw more people into the woods. Not exactly what they're going for. So, we take care of our own. We send them in and we go and find them after."

"But why your parents would let you do that? If they truly believed in all of this, why expose you to it?"

"Because I'm a Bell. It's my responsibility to look. To know. And to fight on anyway."

Mina had a suspicion she was quoting someone but didn't dare to ask who.

"We found her," Basheba continued. "Not too far from here, actually. Just a couple of miles. Katrina had used their bodies like art supplies. She cut them up, nailed them into trees. Let their organs drape down like Spanish moss." She suddenly bolted upright. "A totem pole! *That's* what she was going for. How did it take me so long to get it? Well, now I just feel dense."

Mina kept her silence, twisting her numb fingers together until they hurt. The laughter that slipped past Basheba's lips made her cringe. It didn't last long, though.

"That was the first time I saw my dad break. He couldn't handle seeing his little girl like that. Mom was waiting for us at home. I didn't want her to go through that, too. So, I volunteered to climb up and pull out the nails. I never knew how many organs were in a human body. It took forever."

Mina watched the emotionless girl for a long moment. "How old were you?"

"Are you actively trying to miss the point?"

Before Mina could reply, the smaller girl continued.

"Let me spell it out for you. No matter how bad you think of me, your family is worse. Your daddy *chose* to keep you ignorant. He did that. And then he had the balls to get enraged when I reminded him I'm not just cannon fodder for his crotch goblin's survival."

Mina bristled but picked her words carefully. "You don't seem to have this opinion of Ozzie."

"You and Ozzie are in completely different situations. It was his mother's intervention, not Percival's choice, that kept him ignorant. Also, he just saved my life. That kind of endears me to him a little bit."

Suddenly, Basheba turned to her. Being the sole focus of the smaller girl's attention made Mina's insides twist sharply.

"You know what you're like? You're like that jerk who has never been assaulted, but thinks he has the knowledge to educate rape survivors on how they should handle their trauma. The kind who refuse to admit they're wrong no matter how much evidence is piled up before them."

Basheba lifted her hand to keep Mina silent. "We've barely known each other for forty-eight hours, and you don't hesitate to ask me incredibly personal questions. What? Like it's my job to educate you? To convince you? God, you are like your father. But what really gets me is the fact that it doesn't matter what I say, you're never going to believe me. Even now, after everything you've seen, after everything I've told you, you've still got your cute little nose up in the air. Just biting at the bit to explain to me that I'm just too stupid to understand what's really going on."

Chest heaving and color filling her cheeks, Basheba blinked thoughtfully. "Huh. That makes you more repulsive than me, doesn't it? I mean, I set a high bar, but you might have just climbed over it."

Mina hadn't realized she was hugging herself, twisting her arms around her torso until they crushed the air from her lungs. She could feel her brain melting into slush under the weight of Basheba's accusation. The horrors she had seen. The sound of bees still lingering in her memory. Under the blonde's watchful gaze, Mina felt everything she knew about herself dissolve into a putrid ooze, dripping away to better mirror Basheba's opinion of her. She didn't know if she'd ever see herself the same way again.

***

Why won't they stop shaking?

Ozzie's gloves had been too wet to wear. But, without them, his fingertips had long since gone numb, leaving nothing behind but a deep, throbbing ache. He stared at his hands, ordered them to stay still. It didn't do any good.

Just stop shaking!

Stumbling over the stones and through the underbrush must have disturbed Cadwyn because the older man inched closer to his side, approaching him like he was a startled animal. After a moment of hesitation, he placed a hand between Ozzie's shoulder blades. He knew the contact was coming but still couldn't stop himself from flinching.

Ozzie shoved his trembling hands deep into his jacket pockets, not wanting the older man to see his weakness, but knowing it was too late.

"I'm not afraid," Ozzie blurted out.

"I am," Cadwyn replied. "The last thing I want to do is go back to that tree. I'm glad you're keeping me company."

Ozzie tried to narrow his eyes but couldn't help smiling. "Yeah, I bet you're glad it's me."

"Why wouldn't I be?"

He shrugged. "No offense, but I'd feel safer with Basheba. She might actually be crazier than this place."

Cadwyn chuckled, "Yeah, she might be."

"Think we're all going to be like her after this?"

"I don't think anyone is like Basheba," he replied. Cadwyn left his hand on Ozzie's back as he stooped over slightly, trying to catch his gaze.

"You handled yourself really well today, Ozzie."

Balling his fists didn't stop his hands from shaking. He just wanted them to be still, even if only for a second, but his body was determined to out him as the coward he was. Cadwyn's eyes were as kind as his smile. He gestured loosely to Ozzie's pockets.

"It's the adrenaline. Though, that swim probably didn't help."

Having his joke fall flat didn't diminish his smile. He patted Ozzie's shoulder.

"You'll feel better when you're warm and dry with a good meal in your stomach."

I don't think I'm ever going to feel better. Ozzie kept the thought to himself as they continued to trudge over the slush of decaying leaves and gathering snow. All the while, his trembling grew steadily worse. Memories taunted him, playing like twisted home movies in his mind's eye, never dwelling on any single horror but shifting between all they had witnessed. Each flash broke his resolve a little more.

Keep it together Ozzie. Breathe. Don't let them know they're stuck in the woods with a completely useless child.

It was all for nothing. Tears gathered behind his eyes. His throat swelled shut, forcing each breath to break into a snot clogged sob. Holding his breath, he tried to smother the sound. It only made it all the more noticeable when he finally gasped for air.

The first sob hurt the most. Those that followed toppled out of him as an unrelenting force, shaking his shoulders and making his chest ache. Cadwyn quickly pulled him into a hug as tight as their injured, aching bodies would allow. The wall of body heat left Ozzie painfully aware of how cold he was. There was something about that silent, warm comfort that made the tears come faster. Cadwyn didn't comment. Just rested his head on top of Ozzie's and rubbed his back in soothing circles.

"I'm sorry," Ozzie mumbled between his broken wails, shoving his face hard into Cadwyn's chest to try and smother the sound. As if there was still a chance Cadwyn hadn't seen what a complete mess he was. "I'm so sorry."

"Hey, none of that. You did great."

Great? The word rattled around Ozzie's skull, laughing at him as it clashed against the truth of what he must really look like. A blubbering child clinging to the closest thing that would pass as a father figure. Stripped bare of what he thought he was, Ozzie could only confront what lay at his core. He wasn't strong. Wasn't brave. Wasn't invincible and ready to take on the world. He was useless. Pathetic.

I'm going to die here. I'm going to take them all with me.

Cadwyn tightened his arms around Ozzie's shoulders and brought one hand up to cup the back of his head. "I know seeing a demon can be overwhelming the first time. I can't say it gets easier, but it won't be so bad. The shock wears off after a while."

He went through all of this when he was just a kid.

The knowledge mocked him. To know a child confronted the same thing with more bravery than he could now summon. Percival's voice replayed in the back of his head. *He played chicken with a demon, and the demon blinked first.*

"I'm sorry," Ozzie stammered. "I'll get better. I promise. I'll get better, somehow."

"You saved Basheba's life. Your quick thinking and quicker hands made sure we could keep fighting. How much better do you want to get?"

"You don't have to humor me." Ozzie pulled back, roughly wiped the tears from his eyes, and snorted down a few breaths. "I know how stupid I am."

"You're not."

"It was the first challenge and look at me! She broke me, Cadwyn!"

His voice remained calm and serene. "So what?"

Ozzie used the back of his hands to rub at his eyes again. No matter how many times he wiped the tears away, there was always more to take their place.

"What do you mean? Isn't that bad?"

"Ozzie, Katrina and her demons, this is all they think about. They spend every day thinking about ways to hurt people. Of course, she broke you. We're all going to break. Probably more than once. That part doesn't matter."

"What part does?" Ozzie asked meekly.

He hadn't realized he had lowered his gaze to the ground until Cadwyn cupped his shoulder and gave him a small shake. Just enough to make him look up and resume eye contact again.

"What matters is what you do with the rubble. She has no say in that."

He sniffed, "Huh?"

"The Witch can break you, but she can't take anything from you. My brother taught me that." He waited until he knew he had Ozzie's full attention before continuing. "If you don't think you can make it as you are, take the rubble she reduced you to and rebuild yourself into someone who can."

"How do I do that?"

"Let's start by taking a second and getting those tears out, all right? It'll do you a world of good."

At Ozzie's hesitation, Cadwyn nudged his shoulder. "Hey, crying doesn't mean you're weak. It means you gave a damn."

"Your brother tell you that, too?"

"Nah. Basheba's sister." A small, sad smile flicked across his face, but he quickly hid it behind unrelenting kindness.

There was no mockery in it. He wasn't looking down on him or trying to prop him up for his own gain.

"You're just a nice guy."

Cadwyn's eyebrows jumped, and Ozzie realized he had said that last part out loud.

"Sorry, it was passing through. I didn't mean to sound weird or creepy."

"Ozzie," Cadwyn chuckled. "Do you remember where I work? That's the least creepy compliment I've had in a while."

"What's the creepiest?"

"They mostly revolve around my teeth."

Ozzie sniffed. "They are nice teeth."

"Thanks. They're fake."

The short burst of laughter reopened the dam of tears waiting to be released. He crumbled, both mentally and physically, trusting Cadwyn to catch him. Without a word, the taller man held onto Ozzie and let him cry.

Chapter 16

The sudden thrashing of a nearby bush shattered the silence that had fallen over the girls. A startled scream escaped Mina as she scrambled toward the teepee fire. An instant later, Basheba was crouched by her side, a hunting knife clutched in her delicate hand. They shared a quick glance before refocusing on the shaking plant life. Mina's heart hammered against her rib cage as she tried to steel herself for what was coming for them next.

The bush ripped in two as Buck leaped through it, a bloody mass clutched in his jaws and tail wagging with victory.

Basheba was grinning before Buck's paws hit the ground. She reached out for him, drawing him closer with a rush of praise and excited baby talk. The studded armor was still strapped to his muscular body, but he didn't seem to feel the weight. Bouncing around like a boastful puppy, he rushed over and dumped his prize at Basheba's feet. Blood instantly began to trickle from the broken mass and pool around the mangled corpse, catching the snowflakes as they drifted down. Basheba reached past Mina to stab the lump.

"What did you bring me, baby boy? Huh?"

It hung limply from the long blade, twisting slightly as she lifted it up to the firelight for closer examination.

"Is that a rabbit?" Mina asked.

"New England Cottontail. We're going to eat well tonight." Her voice took on an almost giddy tone as she pulled Buck into a one-armed hug, either expertly avoiding the spikes or ignoring their sharp bite. "Who's the cutest, smartest, best boy in the whole wide world?"

"Okay, now I know that's got to be me," Cadwyn said as he stalked out from the gathering darkness.

"Nope," Basheba dismissed.

He jabbed a thumb to the shorter boy trailing a step behind him. "Ozzie?"

"No. But I do like him more than you at the moment."

Ozzie's chest puffed up a little. Or perhaps it was just that he straightened out of his miserable, defeated slump.

"You do?" he asked.

"You saved me. And you got the bag."

"Hey." Cadwyn tossed the pack to Mina. "I helped."

Basheba slipped past the tall man to her carefully organized cooking utensils.

The boy noticed the clothes warming on the makeshift rack and gratefully changed. It wasn't easy changing under the sleek thermal sheet without losing it, but Mina was determined to make it work. While the rest of the group shuffled and hopped awkwardly about, Basheba busied herself retrieving a pair of latex gloves from Buck's saddlebag, yanking them on, and examining the rabbit.

Mina paused.

Is it okay to eat a rabbit from the Witch's Woods?

"You guys even warmed our socks?" Cadwyn said happily.

"You are awesome," Ozzie said, sighing with contentment as he pulled on the thick wool.

The leather of the collar and cuffs had worked with the river water to rub Mina's skin raw. Still, she didn't dare to take them off as she struggled to pull her sweater on. Somewhat sheepishly, she mumbled.

"That was Basheba. She set up everything."

By the time they had all gathered around the flames, Basheba was ready to reduce the once living creature into a meal. Mina wasn't a squeamish person. She had proven that to herself on the hillside with Cadwyn. But, for some reason, seeing Basheba cut into the little bunny churned her stomach.

The older girl had cleared a stone and stretched the rabbit out on its back with its ears pointed toward her lap. The ever-present mist was somewhat held back by the fire and, as the others crowded around for warmth, she went about her work with clean, efficient, confident motions. The first small cut into its stomach brought a weak beading of blood and a puff of steam. Mina couldn't look away as Basheba worked her fingers in to pry the wound wider. It wasn't because the scene horrified her, but because the fresh kill must still have had some warmth to it. Her frozen fingers ached with jealousy.

Basheba plucked out some small organs and brought them closer to the flames, turning them over with the utmost care, studying them intensely. Eventually, she smiled.

"And to the victor goes the spoils," she said and offered them to the grateful dog.

It was the gulping wet smacks that finally drew both boys' attention. Ozzie's jaw dropped. Mina had never so clearly seen the color drain from someone's face. It didn't matter that he instantly looked away. His nose wrinkled and he started making small, gulping noises.

"Ozzie?" Cadwyn asked in a whisper. "Are you feeling okay? You look pale."

"Why are you killing a rabbit?" Ozzie asked just shy of a whimper.

Basheba didn't pause in her motions, "I'm not. It's already dead."

"But we have other food," Ozzie protested.

Confusion crossed Basheba's face and her hands finally stilled, if only for a second.

"No one told you?" Shrugging off her own question, she gestured a bloody finger to the backpacks. "Check the food."

Curiosity put Cadwyn into motion, the other two following. It didn't take long for him to pull out a clear bag of mixed nuts. He weighed it in his palm for a moment before the lines in his brow deepened and he threw Basheba a quizzical glance.

"Give her a second," Basheba dismissed. "She must be feeling a little lazy."

Opening the pack, he tipped a few cashews out onto his palm, shifting them about with his thumb.

"They look completely normal," Mina said. Plucking one up, she popped it into her mouth.

It turned to sludge on her tongue. A thick, tacky slime coated her mouth, ensuring the taste of rancid meat would linger even after she spat it out. Beside her, Cadwyn made a few disgusted grunts, signaling to her that the other nuts had rotted the same way.

Focused on gouging the innards out of the rabbit, Basheba didn't bother to look up as she spoke. "That's one of her favorite tricks."

"Then why do we keep bringing food along?" Ozzie stuck out his tongue and scoured it with his fingernails after tasting one himself.

Finding her water bottle in her pack, Mina rinsed her mouth out and passed the bottle to Ozzie.

"Wishful thinking, I guess," Basheba shrugged.

Cadwyn dangled the bag in front of his face and poked at the still intact nuts. "She doesn't do this all the time, does she?"

"Katrina likes to mix stuff up," Basheba said.

He frowned and eyed the rabbit with suspicion.

"Will that be safe to eat?"

With a wet squelch, Basheba pulled the rabbit's skin off. "As long as it's not something she created. Its organs looked fine."

Those few words brought hope fluttering into Mina's chest. *There are limitations,* she realized. *If there are limitations, there has to be an internal logic.* It felt like the earth had once again become solid beneath her, no longer crumbling in spontaneous chaos or shifting around her like a dream. There were limits to Katrina's abilities. That meant, even here, in the Witch's Woods, logic existed. Rules existed. Perhaps they weren't the same biology and physics rules the rest of the world had to abide by, but they prevailed in some form, and even Katrina couldn't change that. *If I can figure out what they are, I can find a way to end this.*

Mina clamped her mouth shut before the words could topple free. She couldn't be the first one to ever have these thoughts. Spouting off about them now would only antagonize Basheba and derail their conversation. And she needed Basheba to keep talking.

It struck Mina that she hadn't really been listening. When people spoke, she had been too distracted by her search for cause or reason to simply take in the information. *Observation. Hypothesis. Experimentation.* It had seen her through before, and it would see her through now.

"How can she do that?" Cadwyn asked, studying each of the food bags in turn.

"That isn't the strangest thing that's happened today," Ozzie grumbled, his voice slightly muffled as he crouched low and hung his head between his knees. "I'm still trying to figure out why she stopped with the bees. Why did she let us go?"

Mina's arms curled protectively around herself at the mention of the swarm. Between Ozzie's heavy breathing and Basheba's steady dissection of the rabbit, no one noticed.

"That one's easy," Basheba chirped as she slopped the empty skin aside.

Ozzie gagged.

"There's only so long your 'Thinking Brain' can handle being afraid. After that point, it switches over to 'Caveman Brain,'" she continued.

Cadwyn braved the spitting embers to sit closer to the flames. His obvious fatigue couldn't keep an amused smile from tipping his lips. "I'm going to need you to elaborate on that."

The blonde girl scoffed and started to hack off the rabbit's limbs.

"You can't keep someone in a point of terror forever. If you try, we'll eventually face the threat like our caveman ancestors would have." One solid swipe severed a leg and made the blade clash against stone. "We grab something solid and beat it until it stops moving. That's why she gives us breaks and switches to soft torture methods."

"Soft torture methods?" Cadwyn almost chuckled.

"Right. Sorry. We're supposed to call them 'advanced interrogation techniques,'" Basheba said. "No sleep, hunger, the cold. All that stuff designed to break us down mentally and make the next horror hurt all the more. Katrina likes to alternate between the two."

"That's not comforting," Ozzie mumbled, the firelight making the fine layer of sweat on his face glisten.

"It wasn't meant to be."

"Are you okay?" Cadwyn cut in. "I'm serious. You look really pale."

The teen pressed his lips tight and shook his head, all the while keeping his eyes locked on the dirt between his feet.

"Talk to me," Cadwyn urged.

"Is it the blood?" Basheba asked innocently.

To test her theory, she rocked up onto her knees and reached out, pushing her blood-slicked fingertips into Ozzie's peripheral vision. The boy reeled at the sight, retching violently.

"Blood? Really?" The question slipped Basheba's lips before she huffed gently. It wasn't an unkind sound. "You were fine in the graveyard."

Ozzie swallowed several times in a desperate attempt to stifle his gag reflex.

"Those were burns. It's different."

He barely got the words out before he retched again. Cadwyn was there to rub his back and offer him sips of water. *The aftertaste won't be helping,* Mina thought. It wasn't doing her any good.

"You're okay." Cadwyn's voice was surprisingly soothing. "Just take deep breaths."

Ozzie nodded weakly and obeyed as best he could, spitting a few mouthfuls of water onto the dirt. Keeping his smile bright for Ozzie, Cadwyn swung an arm out loosely toward his medical bag, clearly asking someone to grab it. Basheba raised her eyebrows and her blood-covered hands. Firelight danced off her knife, drawing more attention to the thick liquid that drenched it and the pale skin. Ozzie made the mistake of glancing up and moaned pitifully.

"Sorry," Basheba said and quickly brought her hands back down.

Mina hurried to grab the pack and bring it over. It was a small container of vapor rub that he was after. He instructed the teen to smear some of the sharply scented gel under his nose.

"To block the smell."

It seemed to help a little bit. At least enough that Ozzie was able to sit upright and not look like he was about to faint.

"The smell's the problem? Hold up."

She set the rabbit to cook, messing with the coals to swell the flames. That done, she yanked up a few handfuls of some tall grass. Without shaking off the sticking snow, Basheba used it to clean her hands and tossed the matted mess into the teepee fire. A sweet scent Mina couldn't place quickly tainted the smoke. Ozzie breathed deep and drew one knee up to his chest.

"I'm sorry," Ozzie mumbled. He attempted a weak smile. "I guess I've lost my hero status in your eyes, huh?"

"Start pulling teeth and you'll see me in a worse state," Cadwyn assured him before Basheba could respond.

"Bees," Mina rushed, hoping to distract him and hold off the smaller woman's response. "I'm terrified of bees. Any flying, stinging insect, really."

"Oh. Well, that explains why you were so terrified." Ozzie's eyes widened and he rushed to add. "Not that you didn't have reason to be scared. Anyone would have been in your situation. I just mean..." He stammered for a second before sighing. "I hope you're feeling better."

"Thank you," Mina smiled.

"Drowning," Basheba stated. She barely glanced about the group before fixing her attention on cleaning her hunting knife.

"You're afraid of drowning?" Ozzie asked.

Basheba shrugged one shoulder but it was a tense, jerking motion. "Girls with my name don't do too well in deep water."

Drowning. The word repeated in Mina's head, bringing with it a thickening trail of guilt.

"You handled your fear a lot better than I did." She felt obligated to say it out loud; to publicly admit her weakness.

I'll do better next time. God, I hope there's not a next time.

Basheba's dismissive snort snapped her out of her thoughts.

"That's just practice. And it didn't hurt that I knew it was coming." Using the back of her wrist to push the hair from her forehead left a smear of blood behind. "You won't have such a high opinion of me when she brings out the kids."

"Hold up. Did you just say 'kids'?" Ozzie asked.

"They're terrifying," Basheba said with a shudder. "Especially when you can't see their stupid little faces."

Ozzie glanced around the group, looking about as confused as Mina felt.

"Just to clarify," Mina said as gently as she could. "You're scared of children? Human children?"

"I have a logical aversion to tiny little psychopaths with no impulse control and a limited understanding of empathy."

"So, smaller versions of yourself?" Cadwyn smiled.

She paused, looked at him over the flames, and held her blood-stained hands out in a helpless shrug.

"Terrifying, right?"

***

Curled up on his side, Cadwyn stared at the wall of the tent and tried to decide if it was worth leaving the warmth of his sleeping bag to sneak a cigarette. The heavy snow had set in just as they started their dinner of charred rabbit and apples Buck had brought back from the surrounding darkness. He never thought he'd eat a piece of fruit that had recently been inside a dog's mouth but, by the time Basheba had roasted them over the hot coals, hunger had won out. In all, it hadn't been a bad meal.

Cadwyn had new gratitude for Basheba's nomadic lifestyle. There was fierce independence in everything she did. It allowed him more than enough time to check and treat the numerous small wounds everyone had received, and fix some of his stitches that had popped free. The only chore she had delegated to anyone else was cleaning the dishes. She had kept them far away from any significant body of water. But there was a small trickling stream close enough to glisten in the firelight. It was maybe six inches wide and two inches at its deepest, but Basheba refused to go anywhere near it. No one pushed the issue. The two teens had leaped at the chance to make themselves useful. It took them fifteen minutes to warm their fingers back up after they were done.

Even while she took care of them, Basheba retreated in on herself, ignoring their physical presence as best she could. The only one she never failed to respond to was Buck. He was her constant shadow and, without prompting or reason, Basheba would stop whatever she was doing to lavish the dog with affection. The moments ended as abruptly as they started and were so random that it didn't take long for the remaining three to begin betting on when it would happen next.

Rolling over onto his back, Cadwyn watched as the falling snow deepened the shadows atop the tent. The increasing downfall had brought them inside the tent shortly after dinner, and it hasn't stopped since. It worked with the creeping fog to chase off any trace of warmth. He made a mental note to thank whoever was in charge of selecting the sleeping bags. Heavy-duty thermal was a good choice. It made it all the harder to get up, though. He had forgotten about his cigarette craving as soon as his legs started to cramp. The three-person tent was a tight squeeze for their party. Not at all helped by Buck taking up almost as much room as Basheba did.

He glanced across the row of sleeping bodies. Cadwyn and Basheba had taken to the walls, ensuring the younger two remained protected between them. Buck had coiled around his owner, allowing her to use him as both a pillow and a blanket.

Cadwyn wasn't too proud to admit he was jealous. A big furry animal would be a welcome relief from the ever-deepening cold.

Basheba had stocked the teepee fire just before they had retreated to the tent, and the passing hours hadn't done much to deplete the lashing flames. It made the tent walls glow and accentuated every passing shadow. The idea of having someone keep watch had been tossed around the group but came to nothing when Basheba crawled into her sleeping bag without comment. After a bit of prompting, she murmured that they could do whatever they wanted. *It wouldn't make any difference.*

That comment had lodged into Cadwyn's brain like a splinter, keeping him awake and restless long after the others had fallen asleep.

Does she mean that Katrina will come for us, and we're doomed no matter what we do? The pop and crackle of the flames answered the distant scurrying of rodents. It seemed every sound was sharpened by his clustering thoughts. *Or does she mean that Katrina will keep her distance and let our anxiety get to us?*

Letting his head roll to the side, Cadwyn studied the line of sleeping figures again. He hoped it was the last option simply because it obviously wasn't working on anyone else but him. A small smile pulled at his lips as he watched the others. The fragile peace helped ease his mind. Adrenaline and determination could stave off sleep only for so long. Eventually, staying awake was really no longer an option. The body did what it needed to do and, as his eyelids grew heavy, he realized just how grateful he was for that.

Cadwyn drifted, never fully awake nor truly sinking into oblivion. The cool air invaded his lungs on each breath and trailed down his neck like icy fingers. Small creatures scurried through the undergrowth, and birds let out low, dreary calls. The fire hissed as snowflakes melted against their touch, releasing a woody scent combated against the lingering odor of wet dog.

Tension steadily slipped from his muscles until he felt like he was melting into the frozen earth. He sunk. A distant snap made him flinch, forcing his eyes open, leaving him blinking owlishly at the tent ceiling.

Nothing had changed.

Not sure if he had just dreamt the sound, he looked around while moving as little as possible, not wanting to risk stirring the others. The others breathed slow and deep. Buck whimpered in his sleep, his paws shifting over the tent floor to produce a muffled scrape. Holding his breath, Cadwyn strained to hear anything that didn't belong.

All traces of sleep left him when he caught the distant trace of cackling laughter. His heartbeat kicked up so fast he could barely breathe. Craning his neck but careful not to lift his head, he looked at the others, hoping at least one of them had stirred. Mina and Ozzie had curled up together in a desperate bid for warmth. They effectively blocked his view of Basheba.

Blindly, he slowly stretched one arm out, slipping it over the top of the sleeping teenagers with the intent of tapping Basheba awake. Buck's low growl made him pause. After a moment, he continued. He still couldn't see her or the Rottweiler. The high-pitched laughter came again, far closer than it had been before, and he whipped around to stare at the tent wall behind him. He almost yelped at the first touch. Tiny, chilled fingers crept around his palm, slow and sluggish, the motion of someone still half-asleep.

"Basheba?" he whispered.

She shushed him. The sound barely louder than the chirp of cicadas and the crackling campfire. Her thumb rubbed circles against his palm. That small point of human contact changed everything. All the monsters he had created in his head turned back into shadows. The laughter died away and the placid calm returned. At last, he was able to close his eyes again. Cadwyn curled his wrist so he could take a better hold of Basheba's hand. A branch snapped from somewhere close by. He jerked his head up.

"Did you hear that?" he whispered.

Again, she shushed him. A long, quiet push of breath through her teeth.

Right, don't wake the others.

A part of him wanted to get them up. If something was coming for them, it would be better for all of them to be alert and ready to face it.

Or run.

In the back of his mind, he wasn't entirely convinced he wasn't just being paranoid. The more he questioned himself, the less certain he was that he had heard anything at all. Basheba squeezed his hand reassuringly, and he nodded to himself.

She's been here before. It was a small point but left her in a far better position to survive Katrina Hamilton's Harvest.

It struck him with renewed force just how much security he found in her presence. It didn't matter that he was oldest, biggest, and undoubtedly the strongest physically in the group. Every time he thought of Katrina, he was hurled back through time to become that scared little boy watching helplessly as monsters devoured his brother, mind and soul. Suddenly, he was hyperaware of the music box in the sleeping bag with him. Its pointed edges dug uncomfortably into his spine, but he didn't try to move it. He knew what was gestating inside it, and that knowledge was driving him mad. It left him jealous of the others, Ozzie and Mina in particular. They had had so many years of blissful ignorance.

A sharp snap made him jump, jerking him from his thoughts and thrusting him back to reality. He couldn't pinpoint the exact moment he had dozed off, or how long he had been out, but Basheba's hand was still in his. Soft, cool skin that left him feeling like a giant.

"Basheba?"

Again, her only response was a low shush. Drawing a deep breath through his nose, he forced himself to lay still, and locked his gaze onto the top of the tent. Beside him, Mina rolled closer to Ozzie who groaned at the disturbance but didn't wake up. The air seemed to thicken as he breathed. Tightening his grip on Basheba's fingers, he forced his eyes closed and tried to calm his mind. But the demon's eyes were there, waiting for him in the darkness of his mind. Basheba squeezed back, and he was able to choke down a staggered breath.

Leaves crunched. Tension turned his muscles to stone and his eyes snapped open. *It's just outside.* Keeping his head locked into place, he lowered his gaze to the zipper. The tent walls seemed to pulsate in the firelight, shifting and moving with the collecting shadows. He tightened his grip on Basheba a bit more. Something shuffled outside, and he flicked his eyes to the side, wishing he could see the small woman. Another crunch of dead leaves and a shadow cut over the tent. A dark, dense, foreboding strip of ebony that severed the tent in two. Cadwyn went to lurch up but Basheba's grip kept him down.

"Shh," she whispered on a breath.

Has she been through this before? Did Katrina come do this to her? Does she know what's out there?

Questions sizzled through his panicked mind as the shadow washed over them.

Growing larger or coming closer? He couldn't tell.

His core began to shake, the tremble working into his lungs, forcing him to hyperventilate. Basheba didn't move. Her hand was solid as stone and cold as ice. The small bit of contact was the only thing keeping him from running, from waking up the others, and fleeing from whatever was slowly creeping toward the opening of the tent. It blotted out the firelight, shrouding their shelter in murky darkness as it crept ever closer, each step announced by the decaying plant life. Cadywn clenched his jaw, and held his breath. The silence accentuated every hint of sound. The footsteps stopped right outside. The fabric rustled. His heart slammed against his ribs until his whole body shook with the blows.

Get the kids up! Get them out! Save them! The orders were a deafening scream within his skull, but Basheba's hold on his hand kept him in place. Her stillness became his.

Trust her plan, he told himself. *Whatever it is.*

The zipper rasped as it slowly pulled open. Firelight showed through the opening, seeping around the suddenly diminished figure, washing over the two sleeping teenagers captured in the center of the tent. The shadowy figure loomed inside, and Cadwyn snapped. Slipping loose of Basheba's grip, he jerked upright, a startled scream bursting from his lips.

Ozzie and Mina jolted awake. Buck snapped and snarled. Basheba flung the tent flaps back to fill the space with light and drifting snow. Cadwyn blinked against the glare while his brain struggled to comprehend what was standing before him.

Basheba stood in the entrance, her short stature barely filling the opening even while it cast a colossal shadow. Buck shoved his snout between her legs, still growling, clawing at the dirt as he looked for what had caused the startled cries. Cadwyn snapped around to look at the far side of the tent. Basheba's sleeping bag was empty.

"What? What's wrong?" Mina stammered.

In the same moment, Ozzie also asked what was wrong and Basheba snapped a few profanities.

"What is it? Why are you yelling like that?"

He could only look back and forth between where she stood and where she had been lying only a few seconds ago.

"Cadwyn?" Basheba said sharply. "What's wrong?"

"You were outside?"

Her brow furrowed. "Yeah. Nature called." After a second, she sighed. "I took Buck with me and didn't go far. Promise."

"You were outside," Cadwyn said.

"Yes," she said somewhat sharply. "I'm sorry if I scared you."

Swallowing thickly, he looked down at his hand. He could still feel the chill from her touch. "Whose hand was I holding?"

Chapter 17

Basheba awoke with a jerk. The scent of winter hung heavy in the crisp air and the chill nipped at her nose. Buck's cheeks wobbled as he grumbled in protest. Instead of getting up, he repositioned his head on top of hers and pretended to be asleep. It took a few moments before she could recall where she was. Blinking her eyes open, she found herself the focus of everyone in the tent. Mina and Ozzie looked miserable as they sat side by side to share the warmth of a single sleeping bag. Dark shadows lined Cadwyn's eyes, highlighting the wrinkles that seemed to have deepened overnight. He clutched a mug of tea with both hands and stared at her over the rim.

"Well, this is in no way unnerving," Basheba said softly.

"How were you able to sleep?" Mina countered.

She shrugged, the small motion enough to have Buck protesting again. He looped one paw over her to keep her in place.

"It's a natural bodily process," Basheba offered.

"But, after everything? And then what happened with Cadwyn?" Mina shook her head rapidly like she could fight off the thoughts haunting her.

Basheba gently shoved her pet off her and tried to sit up. Buck had other thoughts and, by the time they were done, he was lounging across her lap, effectively pinning her to the ground with his body weight. Shivering in the chill, she released a jaw-cracking yawn. In truth, it hadn't been much of a conscious decision. She had more collapsed than settled in for a nap.

No good could come from clarifying that now, she reasoned.

Absently, she patted Buck along his snout and resolved not to threaten their fragile morale. Or her own. She looked so much braver when she saw herself through their eyes.

"Katrina's coming for us either way. Might as well nap while you can." Basheba turned to Cadwyn with a smile. "Don't suppose you have another cup of that tea?"

"It's just hot water," he admitted with a small pout. "The teabags have gone moldy."

"There's some spruce trees out there."

He blinked at her, and she explained during another yawn.

"You bruise the needles and leave them to soak for ten minutes," she smiled. "Rich in vitamin A and C."

"How do you know this stuff?" he asked.

She scrunched up her face, "I read. Honestly, it's not that hard."

Breakfast was tense and packing up the camp was not much better. The snow slowed things down considerably. The others tried to help but their lack of experience was almost as bad as the snow. She couldn't believe she was the only one who had ever gone camping before. It seemed like they had missed out on a necessary part of childhood.

Or maybe I was being trained.

The thought bubbled up in the back of her head, bringing with it a thousand different memories.

They had made sure I'd be comfortable in the woods, she realized. A mixture of gratitude and sorrow mixed up her insides until tears pricked at her eyes.

"Basheba?" Cadwyn asked softly as he helped her stow away the tent. "Are you okay?"

"Yeah. Just thinking."

"It'll all be okay."

"I was thinking about good things," she assured him as she pulled Mina's bag closer and started packing things away. "Some good things have happened to me, you know."

"Like what?"

Pushing a sleeping bag down with determination, she lifted her chin. "I got a puppy."

"Okay, I have to give you that."

Basheba's attention wavered when her fingertips brushed against some soft plastic. *More food?* Her stomach rolled at the thought of her sleeping bag getting drenched in the repulsive stench of decay. Yanking it out, she froze, her eyes locked on the little ziplock bag nestled against her palm. *Belladonna.* Katrina hadn't touched the leaves, leaving them crisp and vibrant green. Anger bubbled in her stomach. *Bloody Cranes.*

"Basheba?"

Her head jerked up and her hand closed in a tight fist around the baggie. "Yeah?"

Concern danced in Cadwyn's eyes. "Are you all right?"

"Just missing my morning coffee," Basheba forced a smile and shoved the bag of deadly foliage into the deep pockets of her waterproof hiking pants. "Were you saying anything important?"

"I was just..." He trailed off, the smile on his lips as fake as her own. "Did I cross a line asking about your father?"

Basheba couldn't recall him mentioning any of her family. It didn't matter, though. She wasn't about to tell him anything about her family in detail. There wasn't a lot she had left of them. Just some memories, and a half dozen photographs her uncle hadn't been able to collect first. Logically, she knew sharing these things wouldn't deplete what she had. But logic didn't have much sway over grief. She wasn't about to take the risk. Her memories were her own. Just as her body and her mind were. *And if I can't have them, no one will.*

"Basheba?" Cadwyn asked again, his voice softer than before. Kinder and with distinct hesitation.

"We're wasting daylight."

Brushing aside the gathering snow, she hurriedly zipped up Mina's bag and called the girl over to collect it. Basheba made sure to have her own pack in place and was several feet away before the girl was near. A low whistle brought Buck to her side and she stalked into the woods, leaving the others to catch up if they were so inclined.

The small cluster of leaves in her pocket felt as heavy as lead. It wasn't that she was surprised. It wouldn't be the first time the Crane family had come into the Harvest with this kind of game plan. What niggled at the corners of her mind was how easily she would have ingested the poison. Thinking back, she recalled several times she had accepted bottled water from the Crane girl during last night's dinner alone.

Just because they want to live doesn't mean they care if you do.

She stumbled as the past warning slipped to the forefront of her mind. It had been two years to the day since she had learned that lesson. Sweeping her eyes across the near identical rows of trees, she wondered how close she was to where it had all gone down. Long, silenced screams echoed around her. The coppery scent of blood pricked at her nose.

If I move the leaves, would the blood still be there? There was so much of it. It must have stained the soil red.

"Hey." Ozzie's voice shattered the memories that had shackled Basheba's mind.

She twisted around to watch the group coming closer, still repositioning their packs and organizing their winter gear. Each step came with the crunch of snow and the crackle of frost. Ozzie's blisters had grown enough to give him a small but noticeable limp. *He'd be in a lot of pain if it wasn't for the numbing cold.* A smile pulled at her lips. *Thanks, Katrina.*

Mina eyed Basheba's smile, suspicion plain on her face. "What's wrong?"

"I just need to check the compass," Basheba replied smoothly. "Cadwyn?"

The older man dug into his pocket as he approached and pulled out the small compass disk. It didn't take more than a glance to notice the needle never set on a single spot but spun around at random. Ozzie sucked in a sharp breath.

"Katrina?" Mina asked.

"Magnetic field," Basheba replied. "But I'm glad you're getting into the swing of things."

Ozzie frowned. "What magnets?"

She tried not to laugh at how adorably confused he looked. *Like a little puppy.*

"The hills are filled with nickel," Basheba explained. "Nickel messes with the magnetic fields compasses use to work."

Fear sparked in the depths of Ozzie's dark eyes. "So, we're lost?"

"No."

"I don't mean to argue." Mina's voice sounded a little tense as she spoke the blatant lie. "But we are now without a map or a working compass. How are we not lost?"

"Well, for one thing, the giant mountain that's messing with the compass can help with orientation," Basheba dismissed.

While Cadwyn smiled, he shook his head in a sign of annoyance. "Do you know which way we should go now?"

Basheba pointed in two opposing directions.

"Now you're just trying to be irritating," he said.

"We all need hobbies," Basheba dismissed. "There are two ways to get to the ranch house from where we are now. We go this way," she said as she pointed up the gradually increasing incline, "we'll have to climb up a cliff face that will put an extra day on our trip."

"Why would we take that path?" Ozzie asked.

"It avoids the orchard," Basheba said, stubbornly forcing down the memories that tried to bubble to the surface.

The three people looked at each other and Mina asked, "What's wrong with the orchard?"

Memories pushed hard against her mind's eye. She clenched her jaw and balled her hands in a desperate attempt to keep them out.

"The fruit," she whispered. Swallowing thickly, she carefully bottled the wildfire burning within her soul and searing her mind. Calmer now, she tilted her head to the side, allowing her matted blonde hair to sweep over her shoulder. "No offense, but I don't think you two will do well going that way. Better to fall to your death. Quick and simple."

"That's the way you went before?" Mina asked.

Basheba nodded.

"You survived."

"I was prepared."

Mina smiled. "But we have you and Cadwyn."

"And there's nothing we'd rather do than deal with two teenagers having mental breakdowns in the middle of haunted woods." Basheba watched the girl's polite smile slip. "Sounds like fun."

"How many days do we have left?" Mina asked. "If the detour is going to put at least an extra day onto our trip, how long will we have left?"

Basheba shrugged. "Two. Maybe one, depending on Katrina. The closer we get to the house, the more she can mess with the daylight hours. It makes it harder to keep track of time."

"That's cutting it rather close, isn't it?" Mina asked.

Lifting her chin, she stared at the girl.

"Again, I'm not trying to argue. I'm trying to understand," Mina insisted. "I don't know how long it generally takes to find these keys. Is a day enough?"

She shifted her weight between her feet. "It depends on how well she hides them."

"I suck at hide and seek," Ozzie blurted. "I'm not going to be good at this. I'll need more time."

Cadwyn slipped closer to Basheba's side, hunching over to whisper to the far shorter woman. "I'm not so sure any of us can make it up a sheer cliff face."

Avoiding his gaze, she refrained from commenting.

"*I* won't get up it. Not with this cut on my chest," he continued in a whisper. "And definitely not while carrying Buck's weight, if that was your plan."

Her eyes instantly lowered to the loyal dog sitting patiently at her feet. Leaving him behind wasn't an option.

"I'll take you to the orchard," Basheba said. "But I take no responsibility for what happens there. You all get to carry that yourselves."

Chapter 18

The sun couldn't penetrate the thick blanket cloud cover, leaving the world in perpetual twilight, allowing shadows to shift amongst the trees. Time had turned the fog into a constantly churning mist. Weak enough to see through, cold enough to leave a thin layer of ice over everything it came into contact with. The snow never stopped. Random snaps rang throughout the woods as the overloaded branches cracked from the trunk and crashed down around them.

Despite Basheba's insistence that their ignorance would lead to their demise, she wasn't in any rush to educate them. Mina had struggled to hold her tongue as she watched Cadwyn try and fail to draw the small girl into a conversation. The task was made all the harder since she couldn't get a firm read on Basheba's motives. At first, Mina had been confident Basheba harbored a real and honest fear of the place. But, as time passed, and she still refused to talk, Mina started to suspect it wasn't the only reason. Nor was it just another example of her frigid nature. *Something's changed.* Mina couldn't pinpoint what it was, exactly. But her gut told her it was significant. And that worried her.

Time passed slowly. The cold and her gathering hunger made the trip all the more uncomfortable and, by the time Basheba started to slow down, Mina was glad she wasn't facing a climb at the end of the trudge. Just when she thought she couldn't walk another step on the frozen stumps that were once her feet, Basheba let them take a break.

Ozzie dropped into the mist, slumping onto his back like an upturned turtle. While his antics made both Mina and Cadwyn chuckle, neither decided to join him, and instead found a large stone that could keep them above the mist. Basheba gave her spot to Buck, using his elevation to more easily scrub at his neck in a playful way. The dog's muzzle was white with frozen slobber.

"How deep is the snow?" Basheba asked Ozzie without looking at him. "Just show me with the length of your finger."

Obediently, Ozzie shoved his hand down. "Goes up to the middle of my palm." Repeating the motion a few times, he decided to stand beside his first declaration.

"Good. Take off your bag."

Ozzie flicked his gaze to Cadwyn, waiting for the older man to give an approving nod before he started to struggle free of his pack.

Does he feel the change, too?

In a small act of mercy that she felt endlessly grateful for, Mina found her water bottle hadn't frozen over. She took a few mouthfuls before offering it around. Basheba eyed the bottle for a second before meeting Mina's gaze. Without a word, she turned back around and resumed working on Ozzie's pack, sliding the tent's collapsible metal poles free.

Confused, Mina wondered what the woman's problem was. Basheba's expression had seemed to hold some kind of meaning, but she didn't know how to interpret it. Then it dawned on her. She had been messing with Mina's bag earlier, putting their supplies away. Was there really belladonna there? Had Basheba found it? It would certainly have explained the woman's preoccupation.

But perhaps I'm reading too much into things. Maybe she's just distracted by the forest and being her antisocial self.

Still, Mina couldn't shake the suspicion and waited fretfully until Cadwyn was busy checking Ozzie's blistered feet to move over to the smaller woman.

"Is something wrong?" she asked quietly, almost dreading the answer.

Basheba glanced up at her, her face scrunched up and brows knitted.

"I mean, you seem tenser."

"Do I?"

"Is there anything you want to tell me?" Mina tried again, wanting to get the confrontation over with but dreading it at the same time.

A tiny smile tipped the edges of her mouth. "Like what?"

The conversation was broken as the boys came over. There wasn't much left to eat, and they quickly went through the few berries Basheba pointed out. With that done, it was wordlessly agreed that they wanted to get moving again, to get the horror over with. For once, it was Basheba holding them back. She finished tying the poles to the side of the bag. Then, she worked to loop the ends around the spikes on Buck's armor.

"Shake."

The dog flopped around, successfully knocking the poles aside.

"Good boy," she cooed, completely ignoring everyone else so she could focus on her dog.

"What are you doing?" Ozzie asked when no one else did.

"I'm not going to let him get stuck with your pack if things go wrong," Basheba said.

"He's taking my bag?"

"It won't bother him." She finally paused in her gushing affections to throw a glance over her shoulder. "You can barely walk."

The small act of kindness caught Ozzie off guard. "Thanks, Basheba."

The tiny woman scoffed. "Buck's the one doing the work. Aren't you, pretty boy? Such a good boy."

The group used Basheba's distraction to check in with each other and drink a little more. Eventually, the blonde remembered what she was doing and set off. Once again, it seemed she didn't care if anyone noticed or followed. Buck trotted happily alongside his master, unconcerned with his armor, or the heavy pack now attached to it.

"Were you planning on switching our bags later on?" Ozzie asked, hurrying to clarify. "Cadwyn and Mina could probably use a break as well. And you, of course."

"I think Mina will want to keep hold of her bag," Basheba said with a light giggle.

The guys threw her some questioning looks, but she shrugged, attempting a confused nonchalance. Mina suddenly felt queasy.

She found the belladonna. She had to have. I can't believe my mother actually put it there. She honestly wanted me to poison these people.

Mina wasn't sure what made her feel worse; her parents pushing her to murder, or Basheba believing she was capable of going through with it. *Oh god,* the knowledge was a punch to the gut. A burst of pain that left her breathless. *Basheba thinks I planned to kill her.* Images of the graveyard flashed across her mind. The blonde had almost poisoned the town population because she *thought* they *might* be turning a blind eye. *What would she do to someone whom she thinks is a clear and present threat?* Gulping down the blossoming fear, she followed the others in silence.

The tiny woman always knew where she was going. She wove their way amongst the trees, working over the rolling hills and across moss-drenched creeks as if she was following a map only she could see.

A deep, bone-aching exhaustion had taken hold of Mina by the time Basheba let them rest again. Keeping to the base of a hill kept them somewhat protected from the snow and growing winds. Without discussion, Mina, Ozzie, and Cadwyn clustered closer for warmth. To absolutely no-one's surprise, Basheba favored her dog, instead.

Hunger bit at her insides like a wild animal. Mina spent the vast majority of her break trying to find the perfect way to ask Basheba to send Buck on a hunt. She didn't know how much time had passed but they seemed to have plenty of daylight left. Even if she was wrong, she would be deliriously happy to simply spend a few moments beside a fire.

Before she could decide how best to ask, Basheba let go of Buck and started fussing with the bags again. This time, she retrieved a thin cord from the tent and proceeded to slash her mud-stained shirt into strips.

"Okay, we're going to kindergarten the hell out of this," Basheba said abruptly. "Everyone holds onto the cord. You do not let go of the cord. You do not stop walking."

Oddly enough, it was their silence that finally made her look at them. The large hunting knife in her hand added an extra unsettling element to her glare.

"Am I talking to myself?" Basheba asked.

The three of them hurried to retroactively agree with the requirements. Cadwyn was the only one who ventured to ask questions.

"What's going on with your shirt?"

"Well, I can't trust any of you not to look. So, I'm making blindfolds."

His brow furrowed. A silent sign of confusion that somehow earned him Basheba's full attention.

"I already know what's on the other side of the hill. You don't have to. So, just hold onto the cord and trust me to lead you through."

"I don't like the idea of making you face whatever this is alone," Cadwyn said. "That's the only good thing about this whole setup. We'll all come out with *shared* trauma."

Basheba straightened and passed him the far end of the cord. "Oh, *now* you're all about sharing? Once the pretzels are gone?"

"Are you still not over that?" he asked, taking the cord more out of reflex than conscious thought.

"Cadwyn, years from now, when you're old and gray, and on your deathbed, I will still be berating you over those pretzels. Your poor grieving wife is going to be so confused."

"Huh," Cadwyn said. "You'd think she'd be used to you by then."

"You'd think. But she's very slow. Pretty, but slow."

Cadwyn shrugged. "Can't wait to meet her."

With that, he began to get everyone into position. Basheba, Ozzie, Mina, with him at the rear. Mina wondered if he had noticed Basheba's increased dislike of her and wanted to keep them separated. She was a little surprised when Basheba trusted everyone to tie their own blindfolds.

"Can we at least get up the hill before we put them on?" Ozzie asked. "I'm not that great walking in snow. And if I fall now, I'm taking you all with me."

"We'll go slow," Basheba promised. "Don't worry. It's not for long. The ranch house is right on the other side of the orchard."

Since that was the closest Basheba seemed to come to offering actual reassurance, no one was quick to brush it aside. It was Cadwyn who checked their blindfolds were set in place before Basheba started to walk.

True to her word, she went slow, inching their way up the hill at half the pace she had been forcing them to adopt all day. That changed once they were down the other side. Unable to see heightened Mina's other senses. The wind bit her harder. The crunch of frost and snow was louder. She finally noticed the increasing lingering stench.

The ground had been flat under her feet for a while before the sound of rustling leaves once again surrounded them. Here, however, the sound was riddled with the creak and groan of swaying branches. Her nose wrinkled as the air grew sweet and musky at the same time. The combination brought to mind rotting meat and mothballs.

Even though they all walked in a singular line, it was easiest to keep track of Buck. His makeshift sled created a tell-tale scrape. Everyone else faded into nothing more than footsteps.

Lingering between sensory deprivation and overload, Mina could almost feel her curiosity welling up inside of her, filling her skin and drenching her mind.

They kept walking. A single, slow line trailing through a self-imposed night. The smell grew stronger while the sound of struggling branches became numerous and loud. Mina twisted her hand around the slender cord. Resentment seeped into her curiosity to create a thick sludge in her lungs. It made it hard for her to breathe. Paranoia pricked at her thoughts, whispering that there was nothing around them, that all of this was just Basheba's way to punish them for whatever unknown crime she was blaming them for.

What can she stand to see that I can't handle? Her hand twitched with the desire to take a quick peek of her surroundings.

No one would know. Just one little glance. She pushed it aside only to have a voice whisper, *how do we know she's not leading us to the Witch? She was the only survivor of her last group. Maybe this was how she did it. Offered everyone else up, and killed them herself. It's what my parents wanted me to do after all. She might not be any different.*

The gathering thoughts got the best of her, and she hooked one thumb under her blindfold and peeled it back.

Sunlight, as weak as it was, blinded her for a moment. She squinted around, trying to make sense of what she saw. Everywhere she looked, tall apple trees stretched out to the horizon in perfect rows. One after the other, each loaded heavily with bleeding lumps. A heartbeat later, she understood what she was seeing.

Bodies.

They dangled by their feet, plump and discolored, soft and malleable, like rotten fruit. Snow clung to the blood that dripped from them to create small pools of red around the trunks. A soft groan drew her horrified gaze. One of the nearest bodies twisted in the breeze to bring its rotten, distorted face into view.

Shock hit her like lightning. Death hadn't distorted the face enough that she couldn't recognize her own cousin. Once she had seen one, there was no way to stop seeing the others. One after another, then all at once, she saw the faces of her missing relatives. The ones she had heard whispers about. Those who had come to the Witch's Woods and had never been seen again. And the others. Those whom she had never met before but could *feel* the Crane blood lingering in their veins. And still others who weren't of her blood. Somehow, she could instinctively pick them out. Winthrop, Seawall, Bell. They all crowded the branches. Hundreds of people. Thousands. Twisting and swaying in the snow-speckled breeze.

Mina's jaw dropped but she didn't scream until her cousin's eyes snapped open and focused upon her.

Chaos broke free.

Cadwyn and Ozzie tugged off their eye masks. The added attention woke the corpses. Death rattles filled the air as, one after the other, the bodies turned toward them. Rotten hands clawed at the air in a desperate attempt to reach them. Buck went wild, his thrashing dislodged the pack from his spikes. Basheba tugged harshly on the cord only to have it slip through their hands.

"Run!" she roared.

Hard shoves sent them into motion, but the damage was done. The writhing bodies around them were already tearing themselves free from the trees. Most couldn't stand. Crippled and riddled with decay, the corpses dragged themselves along the ground, moving to cut the living off as they sprinted down the narrow path between the rows. Blood bubbled up from the ground, staining the snow and shining through the mist. Ozzie's panicked cries gave way to panted breaths and whimpers. Mina grabbed his hand and urged him on as the orchard disintegrated into a bloody mush. His hands squeezed hers to the point of snapping bones. When he fell, he took her with him.

Chapter 19

The drop was short and came to a sharp end with a sickening snap and an explosion of pain. Ozzie clutched his arm, instinctively drawing it closer to his body. He could feel his right collar bone shift, the broken edges scraping together, and almost blacked out with the spike of agony. Mina landed on top of him. She rolled away quickly, and he got his first good look at the world around him.

The orchard was gone, replaced by a dark tunnel gouged into the earth. Holes riddled the roof, allowing snow and blood to drift down into the abyss. The screams of the others came down with the debris. He couldn't see them, but he was sure Basheba and Cadwyn hadn't followed them into the pit.

Buck's head emerged over the rim above his head, barked a few times, and then disappeared. He was about to call him back when he noticed Mina's whimpering. It had been lost under the carnage of other sounds above him. Peering into the murky light, he caught sight of her huddled in the shadows. Curled into a tight ball, she pressed her forehead against her knees, clenching her muscles tight to try to stop herself from shivering.

"Hey, Mina, are you hurt?"

"I shouldn't have looked," she whimpered.

Ozzie had barely gotten a glimpse of the hanging bodies before everything had gone to hell. He forced himself not to think about it now, sure that whatever was lurking on the edges of his conscious awareness would cripple him. *What would Cadwyn do?*

"Mina, can you walk? We need to keep moving."

Almost instantly, evidence of this toppled down from the sky. The living corpses had found the openings in the earth and, compelled by their desire to reach them, had hurled themselves into the open air. Their sun-bleached bones shattered as they landed and destroyed their decomposing flesh. It only slowed them down.

Ozzie gripped Mina's shoulders, remembering a moment too late the amount of pain the motion would cost him. "We have to move. We have to get back to the others."

Mina lifted her head, her eyes widening when she saw what surrounded them.

"What is it? What's wrong?" he asked.

"It's too small."

The space was narrow, but not crushingly so. It was almost the same as walking under the low, hanging trees in the forest. But the walls changed everything. They pressed in on them, deepening the shadows and making everything seem smaller.

"Mina, it's a trick." Hearing his own voice made him cringe. Even he wouldn't believe that lie.

She looked at him, though, so he pushed on.

"It's the Witch, Mina. She's just messing with your head. This place is huge."

"Huge?"

The bodies were piling up, creating writhing, festering mountains that inched ever closer to them.

"Godzilla could stroll through without having to duck."

Dead fingers gouged at the soil by his foot.

"Mina, we have to go. I need you to move." He shook her slightly, forcing her to finally look him in the eyes. "Please, Mina."

Her wide eyes locked onto his. While the panic remained, her body stilled. Sucking in a deep breath, she clenched her jaw, nodded once, and got to her feet. A hand latched onto Ozzie's ankle, gripping tight enough that its fingertips popped like rancid grapes. Frantic screams ripped out of him as he kicked his leg back, desperately trying to dislodge the hand, but only succeeding in dragging the corpse along with him. Mina darted forward. She stooped down, driving the heel of her boot into the brittle bone and snapping it in two.

Ozzie snatched the limb up, narrowly avoiding the other hands that burst free from the squirming pile of flesh. The crude weapon felt light and feeble in his hand; nearly worthless, but better than nothing. Tucking his injured arm protectively against his stomach, he lashed out, swinging the limb like a club. He couldn't put the strength he wanted behind the attacks; his body wasn't capable of it. Still, the severed arm collided against the others with a resounding, reassuring crack. It didn't stop the encroaching tide of bodies. Knocking back one only left room for more to follow.

"Can you see a way out?" Ozzie asked Mina, stomping and kicking and swinging.

Mina's back bumped against his as he retreated. She had collected a leg bone from the mush and, together, they carved out a few feet of clear space.

"Maybe if we can get to the top," she said. "Can you climb?"

The thought alone brought a spark of agony.

"I don't think so." Bones shattered under his feet as he kicked a corpse back. "Maybe I can try."

A swift kick from Mina's boot severed a head and sent it soaring into the distant shadows. Watching the motion brought their attention to the clumps of dirt that toppled down from the opening. The horde of corpses fell into such sudden, intense silence that Ozzie heard each clump squish as they landed. He glanced to Mina, barely catching her eyes before the light began to die. They both snapped their heads up to see what had blocked the light.

Spider legs slipped around the edges of the hole, the tips sinking into the raw earth as its colossal body rose up and blotted out the sun. The opening was nearly ten feet in diameter, large enough for an elephant to fall through. Yet the earth ripped away in clumps as the spider surged down, its bulbous abdomen sealing the hole like a cork. Ozzie knew he was screaming. His legs gave out, and he fell upon the still corpses. Tears scorched his eyes. But it all felt beyond him—a distant notion that he could never really be a part of.

Only the monstrous spider was real.

Its exoskeleton clicked as it scraped and struggled. Eyes like glistening black orbs filled his vision. The air became saturated with a choking chemical smell as venom seeped from the spider's sword-like fangs to splash over the corpses. They bubbled and melted upon contact. Weak sunlight blinded him as the creature reared back. The earth fell like rain as it threw itself back down, its large abdomen striking the rim again.

"Ozzie!" Mina cupped his head with both hands. He couldn't see her. "Ozzie!"

She jerked him sharply, nearly tearing the tendons of his neck but forcing him to meet her gaze.

"Stay with me," she begged him. "I can't do this without you."

A shower of dirt rained down on them; the spider was a few feet closer. They threw themselves away from the flailing limbs that shredded through the clustered bodies. Bone, flesh, and rotten organs joined the airborne mud, becoming shrapnel that slammed into their backs and tripped their feet, bringing them back down. Ozzie screamed as he landed hard on his shoulder. Mina's gloved hands caught his face again.

"It's okay. It's okay," she repeated.

He tried to look at the charging spider, but she held his head in place, forcing him to see only her.

"I can't," he whimpered.

"It's like the bees. Just an insect."

"We're trapped."

Cracks snaked through the earth, connecting to the nearest hole and threatening to bring it all down upon their heads.

"It's just a bug." The words left her mouth with a robotic edge. It was something she had obviously repeated to herself until the words had lost all meaning.

What would Basheba do? The answer slammed into him with a physical force.

"Bugs can die."

Mina's eyes widened as she realized what he was suggesting. One trembling hand left his face to wrap around the severed leg she had used as a weapon once before.

"We go for the underbelly," she whispered.

He could barely see her through his hot tears. They dripped free when he nodded. A spider leg swung down and forced their hand. After scrambling away from the path of destruction, the world opened up and the spider dropped into the pit. Side by side, they charged, primitive weapons in hand.

The bulbous end of the spider slammed against the walls as it tried to turn and strike. Each motion ripped apart the dirt confines. Ozzie jammed the broken bones through the small gaps between the exoskeleton. Mina slipped past to do the same to another limb. The dual attack forced the arachnid to sway and slam against the wall of the pit.

Feet slipping through the mud, Ozzie rushed forward, spotting Mina in his peripheral vision. The spider countered and struck; forced them to retreat and reposition. Terror exploded within every cell of his being but he forced himself to go in over and over again. His mind fell away. There was no time for thought.

Suddenly, Mina stabbed its abdomen with the broken edge of the bone. The shell cracked, releasing a green sludge. The spider whipped around, fangs splashing the walls with venom, and struck out at her. Ozzie lunged forward, adrenaline giving him the strength needed to sink the splintering bone into its underbelly.

Mucus rained down upon him. The spider trembled and reared. Droplets of venom sloshed over his wounded right arm and instantly began to eat away at his jacket, working down to his skin. He stabbed again. Again. Cracking the outer shell until he could tear it apart with his hands. Fire burned through his collar bone as he tore out chunks. Mina appeared beside him, adding to his efforts, creating a downpour of sludge and innards. Something sleek and metal brushed against his fingertips. Ozzie caught the briefest glimpse of a wrought iron key before, with a final tremor, the spider collapsed on top of him.

***

Basheba's lungs burned as she sprinted toward the ranch house. Buck ran before her, snapping and snarling, carving a path through the corpses for her. Beside her, Cadwyn endlessly searched the landscape.

"I can't see them," he panted between breaths. "We have to go back."

"Keep running!" she ordered.

The orchard was crumbling around them. Massive trees toppled, their roots spewing blood as they were ripped out of the trembling earth. Bodies scattered the path. The living corpses crawled over the heaving ground. Immense sinkholes turned the earth to honeycomb, swallowing trees and the dead alike, drawing ever closer to their only path out of the orchard. Cadwyn's arm looped around her waist, wrenching her off of her feet and bringing her along with him as he leaped forward.

He forced them into a roll after the first, solid impact. Encased in his arms, Basheba was somewhat protected from the following jolts, but there was no way to prevent her head from smacking against the ground. Stray stones slashed at her scalp and released hot blood to trickle over her forehead.

When they, at last, came to a stop, the world stilled along with them. Their panting stirred the silence. Calm snow drifted down upon them while heavy clouds muted the surrounding colors. Everything was reduced to dreary smears of their former luster. That, more than anything else, assured her she was back.

Peeking out from under Cadwyn's arm, Basheba stared up at the broken ruins of the Bell family home. Time had stained the white walls a broken, dirty gray. Burrowing insects had eaten away the base, and the ceiling was more moss than tile. What had once been a front patio had long since sunk into the earth, leaving only a few splintered ends to split the ground like ancient tombstones.

"I'm home," she whispered.

Cadwyn's weight lifted from her. An instant later, he yanked her up, his hands drifting over her hairline, causing sparks of fire. She swatted his hands aside.

"You're bleeding," he told her.

"I'm fine." Her legs felt weak but held her weight. "Where's Buck?"

"And the others," Cadwyn pressed.

She ignored him as she began to whistle. There was no response. Dread turned her organs to stone. Licking her lips, she whistled again, louder than before. She could feel hysteria digging its hooks into her flesh. Once more she whistled. Silence answered her.

"Buck! Come here, boy!"

"Basheba."

She slapped aside the gentle hand he placed upon her shoulder.

"He made it out with us, right? Did you see him? I need to go back." Biting her lips couldn't stop her ramblings. She called for him a few more times, each repetition growing increasingly desperate. "Buck!"

Warmth flooded her chest at the answering bark. Her weak knees dropped her onto the muddy snow and she lifted her arms, welcoming the Rottweiler into a tight embrace. She took care to spare the dog from her spikey collar and wrist cuffs. His own similarly fashioned armor drove into her skin, but she didn't care. Any amount of pain was worth it to feel him safe and warm within her arms again.

"Are you okay, boy? You had me worried." She sniffed and kissed his snout, unintentionally coaxing him to lick her face.

"Is he all right?" Cadwyn asked.

"Of course, he is. He's the best boy." Her skin felt too tight as she pulled her music box from her straining pocket. Presenting the hated object to him, she instructed the dog to sniff it and gather its scent. "Fetch."

His paws churned up the snow and dirt as he sprinted toward the house.

"You trained him to find the keys?" Cadwyn asked.

"Well, I haven't been able to test it. But he does well finding my favorite beer. And my socks."

Shoving her box back into her pocket, she stripped off her pack and searched for her hunting knife. Cadwyn called for her just as she wrapped her fingers around the handle. The area around the house was a barren patch of dead earth. An empty expanse covered in dirty snow. Knife in hand, she stood, and they suddenly weren't alone.

Children surrounded them. Two near identical rings of prepubescent girls, their dresses as black as midnight, their bonnets as white as the falling snow. She staggered back until Cadwyn took hold of her shoulders and drew her close. Constantly readjusting her grip on the handle of the dagger, Basheba watched as one girl stepped forward. She was the only one who was different. A familiar face in a green dress.

"Katrina." Basheba hated that it came out as a whisper.

A smile stretched the girl's lips as she lifted a hand. A string looped over her palm, leaving a wrought iron key to dangle and sway. Basheba eyed it carefully.

"You're just giving it to us?" Basheba scoffed.

"Only one," Cadwyn whispered.

Katrina's smile grew to impossible lengths.

"You're letting *one* of us go," Basheba said. Using the tip of her knife, she hooked the string and plucked the key free of the witch's grasp.

Katrina let it go, watching the two with obvious anticipation. Passing it blindly to the man behind her, Basheba heard some shuffling and a tell-tale click. *His key.* Her stomach twisted tight. Biting hard on the inside of her cheeks, she tried to keep her face unreadable.

"Go, Cadwyn," Katrina said. "Our game ends here."

Cadwyn shifted slightly, bringing his large frame into Basheba's field of sight.

"And what about everyone else?"

"What does it matter to you?"

His shoulders heaved as he sucked in a deep breath. "I wouldn't be able to live with myself."

Katrina tilted her head. The barely noticeable motion signaled the girls to take a step in, choking off any escape route.

"Can you live with yourself knowing you murdered children?"

He stared at the cube in his hand. It had fallen silent, the pieces now locked in place. Squeezing it until his nails turned white, he spared Basheba a glance before replying.

"You're not kids."

The children surged forward as a pack. Swarming over them, tearing into their flesh, dragging them down to the cool earth.

Basheba didn't hesitate to slash at the little monsters, cleaving large clumps of flesh from bone and leaving the snow stained with blood. She released a sharp whistle, calling for Buck as she struck the nearest child.

At first, Cadwyn tried to keep from hurting the children, shaking them off instead of striking them. But their unrelenting attack soon drained him. His eyes were squeezed tight the first time he used the box as a weapon. He brought it down upon a girl's skull, the sharp edges cracking through skin and bone, leaving a gaping hole for her brain matter to seep out. His fight for life chipped away at his moral hesitation until he struck with a savage brutality that matched the children's.

Sweat gathered under Basheba's thick winter clothes. Her already exhausted muscles struggled to do what she demanded of them. A child latched onto her hair, dragging her down, trying to pin her to the soil, covering her with grasping hands. Buck lurched from behind the wall of children. They buckled under his crushing weight as, instead of pushing through the crowd, he crawled his way over the top of them. Ice replaced Basheba's blood when she lost sight of him. An instant later, she was brought down to her knees. She swung the blade up, driving it into the soft underplate of the nearest attacker.

Cadwyn's screams became muffled. Through the tangled limbs, she spotted him. He had been forced onto his back, his body pinned into place by the combined weight of multiple children, his jaw pried open by the girl upon his chest. Her tiny fingers wiggled into his mouth. A sharp yank and blood poured from between his lips.

With a giggle, the girl examined the tooth she had just retrieved, tossed it over her shoulder, and giddily swooped back in to snap out another. Screaming in agony, he thrashed with renewed force, using the spikes on his wrist cuffs to gouge at their skin. It didn't keep them back for long.

Hands worked under her clothes, clawing at tender skin, searching for her music box. The children had piled on her, grinding her into the now-red snow, ripping out handfuls of her hair and gouging at her cracked lips. The crowd thinned for the barest second as Buck plowed through them. Blood gushed from the girl he held in his grasp. Vicious shakes opened the wounds. The fragile bones of her neck cracked as he tightened his colossal jaws.

Basheba lunged up, taking advantage of the momentary distraction. Slick with blood, the children struggled to keep their hold, and she burst free. They were on her before she could get to her feet, dragging her down again and keeping her on her knees. Every muscle in her body trembled as she forced them to their full strength. With a solid thrust, she grabbed the bonnet of the girl sitting on Cadwyn's chest, wrenched her back, and sliced her throat.

Use had dulled the blade but it still sunk deep enough to sever the artery, baptizing them both in her blood. Before she could see if it was of any help, a heavy weight landed upon her spine and drove her down. Hands pulled at her fingers in an attempt to pry them from the knife handle.

Buck charged. Lowering his head, he used the spikes as a battering ram, forcing the girls back just enough to drop a severed head on Basheba's hand. The soft squish came with a sharp clack against her knuckles. She snatched it up as Buck shredded the crowd. His armor held strong, preventing the small bodies from gouging at his head or back. There was nothing they could do to counter his attack of fangs and pure muscle.

Rolling the head over to look at the mauled flesh of the neck, she discovered a slip of metal protruding out of the cracked spinal column. Prying it out with the tip of her knife, she rolled closer to Buck, using his protection to retrieve the box from her pocket. Sliding pieces exposed a small lock. Bone marrow gathered around its edges as she pushed the key inside.

The lullaby came to life, hollowing out her mind until it was all she could hear. Deafening. Endless. Echoing within her bones. Hands grabbed her arms, trying to pull her away. She twisted her wrist. The key flipped the lock and silence claimed the world.

An arctic chill rushed to meet her flushed skin. The blood remained while the rest of Katrina's creatures scattered like ash. Buck leaped about to snap at the floating particles, endlessly frustrated that he couldn't sink his teeth into any of it. She called him over as she crumbled. An arm around his shoulders kept her somewhat upright. She could barely lift her head as she called out for Cadwyn. Waiting for his reply and hearing nothing sent her adrenaline coursing again. She snapped upright to find the man sitting a few feet from her side. His arm held out before him, his eyes wide and unblinking under a layer of dripping blood.

"Cadwyn," she said gently as she shuffled to his side. Carefully, she placed a hand on his arm. "They weren't really kids. They weren't human."

"We have to wash off before Ozzie finds us." His voice was distant and flat. All the screaming came from his eyes.

Mina's voice broke over his soft ramblings. Snapped from their daze, they looked up to see the two teenagers sprinting from the orchard. Both were covered with thick mucus, but it was the way Ozzie clutched his arm that made Cadwyn shoot to his feet. Ozzie skidded to a stop when he saw them. Basheba was slightly impressed when, after a moment of hesitation, he forced himself on.

"He's hurt," Mina panted. "His shoulder. We found a key!"

Cadwyn shrugged off his winter jacket, turning it inside out to hide the blood before fastening it around him as a sling. With Ozzie in shock and Cadwyn fixated on his task, it fell to the girls to catch each other up.

"You climbed up a dead spider to get out of the pit?" Basheba asked when Mina had finished filling her in.

"That's the part you're stuck on? We found a key!"

"*Ozzie's* key," Basheba explained. "Every box has its own."

It struck them all at the same moment that Mina was the only one left unaccounted for.

"We'll find it," Ozzie promised, pain pulling the muscles of his face taught. "We have a bit more time."

"I don't suppose you want to give us a hint," Basheba screamed to the barren world around them.

She hadn't expected a reply, but one came swiftly. Pain exploded behind her left eye. A blinding, crippling fire that made her knees buckle and her mind sputter. Cadwyn was by her side in an instant, slowing her decent to bring her gently to the ground. His fingers were warm and smeared with blood as he pried her hands back from her face.

"What is it? What's wrong?" Ozzie asked, and offered his good hand to Basheba so she'd have something to hold onto.

"I can't see anything," Cadwyn whispered, clearly not sure if he wanted her to hear or not.

Basheba meant to calmly state that she could feel something pushing against the back of her eye. The words came out as a feral scream that had Buck restlessly pacing beside her. She reached out blindly to soothe him, and he nuzzled her palm. The gentle touch served as an anchor, allowing her to croak out.

"The key."

"She put it behind your eye?" Ozzie asked. "Can she do that?"

"We need to get her to a hospital," Cadwyn said.

"My box hasn't been locked," Mina cut in. "Is it safe to travel through the orchard again if my demon hasn't been properly sealed?"

"I can't handle another spider," Ozzie stammered.

A deep growl left Cadwyn's throat. "I can take her down the cliff."

"I thought you said you couldn't climb it before," Mina said.

"Not with Buck on my back. Basheba weighs a lot less. I can get the key and come back."

"Do we have time for that?" Mina asked.

"You want us to wait here?" Ozzie said. "With the Witch?"

Grinding her teeth Basheba snapped a hand out to grab Cadwyn's wrist. "I'm not leaving Buck."

"It'll just be for a little while."

They all knew it wouldn't be, but it was Mina who voiced the points one after another. Basheba was the only one who knew her way through the woods. They had no supplies. With the incoming storm, the stream Basheba had mentioned could freeze over. Crossing it with an injured girl on his shoulders could be suicide.

"Cut it out." Basheba's order brought tense silence.

Cadwyn stammered until she dug her nails into his arm. The waves of pain had weakened to a near constant but tolerable ache.

"You have your med-kit," Mina said. "Cut the key out and put an end to this."

"In the middle of the woods? While I'm covered in mud and blood? With no anesthetic? And, at best, two days away from proper medical care? Are you insane?"

"You can pop it out." Mina rushed on when Cadwyn glared at her. "You won't have to cut anything."

"But her eye will be outside of its socket!"

"There's every chance she'll keep her vision," Mina argued.

"I'm not putting her through that much pain because you can't be patient."

"You know what's coming," Basheba cut in. "Let's end it here."

Cadwyn shook his head, "This isn't up for debate."

"Is it up for extortion?" Basheba countered. "You pop out my eye, or I'll stab it out."

"We can make it back to town. I know I can do it."

"Cadwyn," she groaned. "The demon isn't the only reason I want to do this."

"What's the other?"

"Spite. Katrina did this because she doesn't think I'll go through with it. She thinks I'd rather leave Mina to die than lose my eye. Well, screw that."

"You can't just do things out of spite."

"It's the only reason I do anything," Basheba countered. Clutching Buck close, she tried to settle herself against the snow, as if this would all be easier if she could just get comfortable. When she shifted her gaze to Mina, she could feel the metal edge rubbing against the back of her eyeball. "You want to be a doctor, right? If he won't do it, try and stop the bleeding."

For once, Mina kept her silence and only nodded.

"Ozzie, don't watch."

"I want to be here for you, Basheba."

"And I don't want you to throw up on me," she replied with a weak smile she hoped was encouraging.

He tried and failed to return the gesture. Swearing constantly under his breath, Cadwyn rummaged through his med-kit for sterile wipes and cleaned his hands as best he could with them.

"You'll have to stop holding the dog," he grumbled.

"If I let go of him, he's going to go for your throat," Basheba said.

Instinctively, she closed her eyes to try and prepare herself for what was to come. Her gut churned when Cadwyn instructed her to open her eyes again.

"I'll do my best."

"I trust you," she whispered.

His hands were shaking as he placed them by her eye. She tried one last time to reassure him with a smile. It didn't work, but he began, anyway. Pain swept through her, consuming her, boiling her within her own skin. Buck struggled against her, trying to break free and save her. She felt the pop just before darkness washed over her and dragged her into oblivion.

Chapter 20

Locking the final box had changed everything. The oppressive cold that had been there since they first stepped into the Witch's Woods was gone. There was still a chill, strong enough to have them huddling together during the night. But the mist had lifted and, without it, the harshest bite of the air had been soothed.

They had lost most of their camping gear at the Bell homestead. When Basheba was conscious, she had instructed them as best she could, but they had all agreed to let her sleep as much as possible, so they were often left to work things out for themselves.

The two-day hike passed in a blur, fatigue, pain, and shock each playing their part to keep their minds dulled. Every time Mina tried to think, all her brain could linger on was the incredible sacrifice Basheba had made for her. A part of her was quick to believe the woman's explanation. Hatred and spite were strong motivators. But in the somber aftermath, with each of them nursing their physical and psychological wounds, Mina didn't think that was the case. Nor was it the noble desire to keep the demon from being unleashed upon them. By the time they had left the Witch's Woods to rejoin the cleared recreational path, Mina was sure Basheba had been motivated by grief. Mina had seen the orchard and felt their lineage. She knew how many Bells hung there.

Reaching the parking lot felt like stepping back in time. Everyone looked exactly as they had left them. Comfortable. Healthy. Safe. Once more, the four families had crammed themselves into the limited area. This time, however, the scent of hamburgers drifted on the air and a few tents had replaced the cars. It looked like a tailgate party.

They were ready for a long wait.

It was impossible to tell who in the mob spotted them first. One cry set up the next and soon enough the clearing was full of life. The excitement only grew as it became clear all four had survived. A few poppers were set off; sharp cracks that rained colorful streamers down upon them. Others threw flower petals; pink and white roses that flipped and twisted before settling on the fine layer of speckled snow.

It's like they're welcoming home heroes.

Mina looked to Basheba, trying to see if this was the standard practice. A yellowed gauze patch covered one eye. The other held more sorrow than fire.

They hadn't reached the parking lot before people flooded up to meet them. Ozzie had to brace his good arm over his wounded one to keep from getting jarred by the flood of relatives he didn't really know. Cadwyn welcomed his mother, holding onto her even when his stitches started to bleed again. Mina looked up in time to have her father and mother almost knock her off her feet.

"Are you hurt?" Jeremiah asked as he joined the group.

Mina shook her head.

"That's my girl," her father boasted, raising his voice louder for the others to hear. "To hell and back with barely a scraped knee!"

Cheers rang out, sounding like an army after the two days of near silence. Mina slowly pulled away from her parents to wrap her brother in a tight hug.

"What happened out there?" he whispered.

"I'll tell you later." She leaned back enough to catch his eyes, wanting him to know the full weight of her words. "You and the others. No more secrets."

He shushed her. "Don't let mom and dad hear you say things like that. We have our traditions."

A booming voice rang out over all the other mirth, drawing Mina's attention. Across the parking lot, Basheba stood with her uncle before the couple Percival Sewall had brought along.

Ozzie's parents, her mind corrected.

The uncle was boasting. Understanding his actual words weren't necessary. It was clear by position and gesture alone that the Bell was raining praise down upon his niece. But he never looked at her. His attention was fixed on the rich couple.

Every muscle in Basheba's body locked tight as her uncle began to play with her long blonde hair. Twisting the strands around his hand until each rhythmic clench of his fist made her arch her neck back. It almost looked like an absentminded sign of affection. An innate desire to maintain some kind of physical contact with the relative he had almost lost. But there was something in it that left Mina unsettled.

She felt it like a coming storm; the moment when Basheba snapped. Mina anticipated that she'd push the older man away. Slashing at his face with her hunting knife wasn't something anyone had seen coming. Shock and horror washed through the crowd. Only four people stood undisturbed.

Four people and a dog.

While the knife had made contact, the man had jerked away in time that the cut on his face wasn't deep. He belatedly hurried to move out of his niece's reach as someone handed him a shirt to press to his face.

"I need to get Basheba to a hospital," Cadwyn cut in smoothly, before the small woman could do more.

"I have a helicopter," Ozzie cut in. "If you guys want a ride."

"Thanks," Basheba smiled, her attention diverted from her uncle.

"I'm coming, too." Mina got three paces before her father tried to pull her back. "Someone's got to hold Buck. I'll meet you at home."

The whole time in the woods, she had wanted nothing more than to be back with her family. Now, she felt like she couldn't breathe.

They knew. They knew about all of this, and they said nothing. Nothing but lies my whole life.

She pushed down the thought just as she had a thousand times before and hurried to catch up. A voice drifted from the woods before they could leave. A sweet, whispered voice that left everyone in tense silence. The voice of the Bell Witch.

"Goodbye. I'll see you next year."

* * *

If you enjoyed the book, please leave a review. Your reviews inspire us to continue writing about the world of spooky and untold horrors!

Check out these best-selling books from our talented authors

Ron Ripley (Ghost Stories)
- Berkley Street Series Books 1 – 9
  www.scarestreet.com/berkleyfullseries
- Moving in Series Box Set Books 1 – 6
  www.scarestreet.com/movinginboxfull

A. I. Nasser (Supernatural Suspense)
- Slaughter Series Books 1 – 3 Bonus Edition
  www.scarestreet.com/slaughterseries

David Longhorn (Sci-Fi Horror)
- Nightmare Series: Books 1 – 3
  www.scarestreet.com/nightmarebox
- Nightmare Series: Books 4 – 6
  www.scarestreet.com/nightmare4-6

Sara Clancy (Supernatural Suspense)
- Banshee Series Books 1 – 6
  www.scarestreet.com/banshee1-6

For a complete list of our new releases and best-selling horror books, visit www.scarestreet.com/books

See you in the shadows,
Team Scare Street